The Diwesh Chronicles

Justice

The Diwesh Chronicles

Justice

C.O. Stephan

Copyright © 2010 by C.O. Stephan.

Library of Congress Control Number: 2010906494
ISBN: Hardcover   978-1-4500-9733-8
                Softcover   978-1-4500-9732-1
                Ebook   978-1-4500-9734-5

All rights reserved. No part of this book may be reproduced or transmitted in any form or by any means, electronic or mechanical, including photocopying, recording, or by any information storage and retrieval system, without permission in writing from the copyright owner.

This is a work of fiction. Names, characters, places and incidents either are the product of the author's imagination or are used fictitiously, and any resemblance to any actual persons, living or dead, events, or locales is entirely coincidental.

This book was printed in the United States of America.

To order additional copies of this book, contact:
Xlibris Corporation
1-888-795-4274
www.Xlibris.com
Orders@Xlibris.com
79102

Dedicated to

My wife and five children

Who never stopped believing in me

CHAPTER ONE

Hans squinted his eyes against the glare from the sun that was low on the horizon as he pressed himself against the rocks, glad that his brown covering blended so well with his surroundings. Positioned between two rocks so he could see without profiling himself against the horizon, he looked down at the sandy shore littered with rocks and boulders. He enjoyed the warmth of the sun on his back as he began a careful survey. He never went to the shore without first spending time checking every feature in the open area. It was too dangerous.

As he scanned the far end of the shore he thought he detected a movement. He quickly looked away and then back again. Yes, someone or something was moving out there. His eyes soon found and followed the figure as it moved along the shoreline. Was he mistaken or was that a Runner? He hated the Runners. They had been nothing but trouble ever since they first arrived. The Rasset had imported them because they were able to cover long distances easily, required little to sustain them, and they had no interest in political affairs. Their thin bodies seemed out of proportion because their long legs made up two thirds of their height. They rarely came to this Zone, so the presence of one meant trouble for someone.

Hans knew he was in no immediate danger. Runners never hurt anyone. They just let the Rasset know instantly when they came across any unauthorized personnel in a Zone. Their job was to find "troublemakers" or people who moved from one Zone to another.

As he watched, the setting sun reflected off a metal sash. It *was* a Runner. What was he doing here? There were only a few thousand people in this Zone and Hans would have been informed if anyone new had come into the area.

He slid his left hand into the slit in the side of his covering that allowed access to an inside pocket and brought out a black glove. Quickly putting it on his right hand, he raised the gloved hand, pointed the index finger, and squeezed the other three fingers into a fist. The flash of light from his fingertip landed right where he intended. It hit the metal sash in the center of the Runner's scrawny chest. The electrical charge knocked the transmission sash out of operation and the Runner was down.

Hans quickly ran to the stunned figure. Because of their lighter bones, a Runner's hairless body was fairly fragile but the stun of the static electric charge would not last for long. He must act before the Runner regained consciousness. He looked at the wedge shaped face that came to a point at the chin, the thin membrane that covered the hole in the center of the face which was its nose, and the overly large eyes that were able to see much from a distance, but very little that was close. That feature had enabled Hans to escape detection more than once. The trick was to stay close to them so they could not see you. The ears were mere openings in the side of the skull and could not pick up sounds easily.

He wanted to get out of the open as quickly as possible so he picked the Runner up and headed back toward the rocks, making sure not to return to the same spot he had been in before. It was a habit he had developed long ago. He never returned to the same location once he had been out in the open and he never used the same place as a lookout twice in a row. As he carried the limp body back toward the rocks, he wondered where this one had been going and who he had been sent to find. Reaching the hollowed out log he had hidden along the stream that emptied into the sea, he placed the limp form in the dugout, pushed it into the main current, and watched as it traveled down the channel and into the sea. He continued watching until the tide caught the log and began to pull it out into the open water. He didn't know where this Runner would end up and he really did not care. He would have preferred killing him, but doing so would have alerted the authorities immediately because when a Runner's heart stopped beating a signal was automatically sent to the Compound that had sent him out.

Hans moved to a new location where he could conceal himself among the rocks again and resumed his survey of the shore. He thought he had noticed something else out of the corner of his eye when he was carrying the Runner—something that just didn't seem right. He resumed his survey of the area; looking for whatever it was that had caught his attention. He took his time; he had to be certain there was nothing out of the ordinary before he left this beach.

As he moved his gaze slowly from the sea to the bank's edge, he examined every rock. Finally, he noticed something that looked wrong with the shadow of one of the larger rocks dotting the shore. Hans could not tell what it was and did not dare stare at it for long in case it was human. He knew all too well that if it was human, it would sense being watched if he looked at it for any length of time. He continued his survey, looking for anything else out of the ordinary. Only after a thorough survey did he move, and even then he kept himself low. He changed his location three times, each time getting closer to the form and each time staying in his new location long enough to be certain there was nothing that did not belong there.

When he arrived at the third location he was close enough to see the object clearly. It looked like a human body. Was this what the Runner had been after? It seemed unlikely because the Runner had already gone past this point when Hans had stunned him.

Still . . . . the body was not easy to spot and the Runner had passed near this location and would not have been aware of anything that close to him due to his long distance vision. Hans had not seen it at first because there were several rocks about the same size in the shadow of the larger rock. It blended in very well—almost as if it had been placed there on purpose so it would not be noticed.

Only after he was certain there was nothing else anywhere on the shore, and that the form was not moving, did he finally approach it. Picking up a piece of driftwood, he crouched down in the shadow of the rock near the unmoving form. He reached out and prodded the seaweed covered shape with the driftwood. Nothing. He circled around it, prodding it several times, always ready for a sudden move. Still nothing. He moved closer to the rock and sat down where no one could see him except from the sea, knowing there would be no one out there in that blue expanse, and watched the form. He studied the body carefully for any indication of life. There was a slight rise and fall indicating it was still breathing.

As the sun sank below the horizon, he went near and used the toe of his moccasin to roll it over. As it rolled, a slim arm flopped into the wet sand, and Hans could see the color of the covering, now that it was not concealed by seaweed.

He was puzzled. Everyone, except the Rasset, Ratona, and Dura—who all wore long purple robes—had to wear a toga style covering and each Zone wore a different color. Whoever this was, they were not from this Zone. Hans had not actually seen a green covering before. He only knew it was worn by those in Zone Five which was located on the other side of the Middle Sea.

"You should just leave and get out of here," he told himself. Knowing full well he wouldn't. He picked up the form, put it over his shoulder, and headed for the cave, anxious to get away from the open and away from an area where a Runner had been sent.

Still careful not to take a direct path, he climbed higher and higher above the shoreline. When he finally arrived at his destination he was glad the body was not any heavier. The opening to the cave did not look large enough for a person to enter because the ground was much higher just in front of the cave than it was right at the entrance.

Stepping down off the higher ground into the cave's opening, and being careful not to bump the body into the rough edges of the small opening, he entered a dark cavern. Without any light, save the dim light of the first rays of the rising moon, he proceeded ahead into the darkness for ten full strides, then turned ninety degrees to his left, took five more strides, then turned left again. Fortunately, he had used this cave often enough to be able to move confidently in the darkness. He reached out and felt the cool, rough stone wall. His fingers searched for, and found, the handle of a torch. Reaching into the pocket of his covering he brought out a match and scratched it against the rough surface of the wall. He held the match to the top of the torch until it began to burn. The light illuminated the darkness enough to reveal an almost circular space about twenty feet in diameter. The ceiling was lost in the darkness.

Laying the body down next to the small fire pit located in the center of the cave, he stirred up the coals to get the fire going again. Only when the logs began to burn did he turn his attention to his burden.

He began a slow, careful examination. The hair was dirty and matted. The covering was torn and ragged. There were bruises everywhere and—it was female.

He walked over to one side of the room to a ledge that was filled with several jars and bowls. He picked up a small bowl, filled it with water from one of the clay jars, and returned to the fire pit where he set it at the edge of the fire to warm up. Then he went to the other side of the cave where there were several small bundles. Reaching into one he brought out a roll of bandages and a small jar of ointment. From another he took a couple clean rags, and from a third bundle he took a clean covering.

Returning to the fire, he began checking the body for injuries. As he carefully felt the skull he found a rather large goose egg swelling on one side.

"Well, that explains why you're such a sound sleeper," he said softly.

Dipping a cloth into the water, he began to wash away the dirt and blood. He worked cautiously, taking care not to open any of the cuts that had stopped bleeding.

As he worked, he wondered just what had happened to her. She was in pretty rough shape. Her hands were cut and badly bruised. Holding one in his own rough hands he examined it carefully. It looked like it had been torn by, or dragged over, rough rocks or something similar. Most of the damage had been to the hands and lower arms. There did not seem to be any damage to the legs or feet. Once he completed the washing, he applied some of the ointment to every cut and scrape he had found.

Only after this was done did he begin cleaning the face. He found she was not unattractive or old—guessing her to be somewhere in her mid twenties to early thirties. She had a small, well-shaped mouth and a finely chiseled nose which was just the right size for her face. He took the time to rinse out her dark hair and try to untangle the knots with his fingers. He remembered how important it always was to his daughter to have her hair looking clean and neat. Even after they had lost everything that was considered "unnecessary" by the Rasset, she had always wanted her hair to look tidy.

Next he untied her covering so he could check for any other cuts or bruises on the body.

"Sorry miss," he said as he removed the covering, "don't want to embarrass you, but I need to know just how badly you are hurt."

It was not until he washed away some mud on her shoulder that he found the circle. Left shoulder. He felt a knot in his stomach tighten.

What was he supposed to do *now*?

"Well little lady, you're not dead yet," he murmured, "and I don't know if you'll make it or not, but I have to do this."

He pulled the razor sharp, eight inch long, double-edged dagger made of the finest Diwesh steel from the sheath that was strapped to his thigh under his covering and cut a shallow slit from one edge of the circle to the other and then another cut to form an "X" crossing right in the center of the circle. Peeling back the layer of skin, he found the round metal disk just under the surface. Grimacing as he worked, he pried the thin disk until he could locate the four thin cords that held it in place. Carefully he cut each one and then removed it. Only after he had all four cords removed did he pull on the disk. He felt the body tense up. The disk resisted for a moment, then came loose with a flow of blood. She let out a moan, and then her body went limp again.

Quickly he folded the skin back into place, applied some ointment, and put a clean cloth over it. He tore a strip from the roll of bandage and used it to hold the cloth in place.

Gently laying the body down on the right side, he went to a recess in the cavern wall and brought back a blanket of sorts. Actually it was little more than scraps of coverings tied together for the purpose of providing warmth.

"Sorry, little lady," he said, "but this is the best this hotel has to offer. I don't require much myself and don't usually bring any guests home with me."

After covering her with the blanket, he picked up the disk and moved closer to the fire. This was only the fourth disk he had ever seen—and the first one from a living body. Turning it over in his hands he noticed about a quarter of it was crushed.

"Well," he muttered, "that explains why you aren't dead yet." He knew the disks were designed to keep track of those they were implanted in and would stop the heart if the "host" was thought to be in danger—or running away.

Placing the disk in a pocket inside his covering, he walked back to the entrance and stood there listening. Only when he was satisfied that there were no sounds except the normal night sounds, did he return to the beach. Soon afterward he returned to the cavern and listened to the soft breathing that seemed to be normal for a sleeping person. He stretched his lanky body out on the other side of the fire pit and prepared to doze. He knew he wouldn't sleep much, there were too many unanswered questions, but he needed some rest. He just hoped she would still be alive in the morning.

CHAPTER TWO

Daylight was just starting to lighten the sky when Hans walked outside to have a look around. He did not dare go far from the cave, but he wanted to make certain there was no danger.

After a thorough survey of their surroundings, he was satisfied there was no immediate danger. Reentering the cave, he stirred up the embers in the fire pit. Adding some small pieces of wood to the fire, he watched as they caught, then he went to another recess in the cave and came back with some moccasins and placed them alongside the clean covering he had set down beside her the night before. He was thankful he always kept an extra covering because, even if her own had not been so torn up, it would have called immediate attention to her because it was not the color for this Zone. Attracting attention was the last thing they would want to do.

He picked up the bowls and jars from the night before and returned them to the ledge.

When he came back to the fire pit, she was sitting up with the blanket wrapped around her, watching him.

"Put that covering on," he said softly, "there was not much left of the one you were wearing. If the moccasins are too big just lace them tighter for now. I'll modify them tonight."

She did not move. Her brown eyes strained to make out details in the dim morning light.

He went back to the corner of the cave and she heard the sounds of packages being handled.

"Aren't you dressed yet?" he said when he returned. "We don't have all day."

"Who are you and what am I doing here?" she asked defensively.

"I found you on the beach and brought you here."

She ached all over. She looked down at her hands. They were cut and bruised but she could move them.

He placed a couple of food pouches beside her.

"Hurry up and get dressed so we can get going."

"What's the big rush?"

"They will start searching when the sun is fully up."

"What will they find?" she asked as she picked up the covering.

"Nothing."

She started to put the covering over her head and the movement caused her to feel pain in her shoulder. She looked at him in fear.

"Don't worry. I removed the disk."

"I didn't think that was possible."

"Normally it isn't. But yours was damaged so I could remove it without killing you."

"Then we don't have anything to worry about," she said as she turned away from him and put on the new covering as quickly as she could. The pain in her bruised body would not allow her to move very rapidly.

"Yes, we do." he replied. "One of their Runners is missing."

She laced the moccasins even though it hurt her bruised hands and quickly put the food pouches he had given her into the pockets of the toga type covering everyone wore now.

When she turned around again, he was gone. Following the dim light of a new day she soon found him standing just to the side of the opening and scanning the horizon.

"Anything?" she asked as she came up beside him.

"Not yet," he replied as he continued to scan every bit of cover there was out there. "But it won't take long."

"Where is the Runner?" she asked.

"Somewhere in the sea," he replied. "I went back after I had cleaned you up a bit just to make certain he had not washed back up on the beach. You really need to learn to take better care of yourself."

She caught the slightest hint of a smile on a face that seemed to smile rarely and responded, "Well, some days a girl just doesn't have time to fix herself up for unknown strangers."

He looked down at her and said "Let's get moving," as he walked outside in the early morning sun.

They started off and she kept up with him even though he set a brisk pace. After almost three hours of steady, silent walking over the gently rolling hills, moving from one wooded area to another, he stopped.

Pointing to a low rise ahead he said, "We'll stop there for a short rest. There's water and a good view of the surrounding area."

She nodded and they continued on. When they reached the rise, she was surprised to suddenly find a wide crack in the ground.

"Hidden canyon." he said as if he were reading her mind. "Only one in this area. Nobody expects there to be one, so they pass by without any idea it is here. Located behind the trees on the south side like it is, and with the mountain to the north, those who travel the road have no idea of its existence."

He helped her down to a ledge about three feet below the rim of the canyon and then climbed down himself. She sat down in the small amount of shade it provided and took out one of the food pouches he had given her. She was surprised how hungry she was.

"You still haven't told me who you are and how I came to be in your cave," she stated as she bit off a piece of the packet and began to chew.

"Well," he said as he sat down just below the rim of the crater so he could look out without being easily seen, "names don't seem to matter much. Besides, you haven't introduced yourself yet either," he said as he raised his left eyebrow.

She noticed that his eyes were two different colors. The right one was a light blue and the left one was a dark green which meant he was a Diwesh. She had never seen one before but had heard about them. *What is he doing so far from his homeland?* she wondered. They were reputed to be fierce warriors and their country was far from here.

"Most people just call me Hans. As for how you came to be in my cave—I carried you there. Always figured anything the sea washed up was mine for the taking if I wanted it. You didn't look like much, but I figured I'd try to make something of you. Maybe I figure to return you to the Rasset."

Her face froze. He wouldn't—would he?

"But," he continued, "when I found that disk I changed my mind."

Again she noticed the hint of a slight grin.

"Why?"

"Because maybe you can help me."

"How?" She was suddenly very wary of this stranger.

"By telling me how you managed to get away from a Compound with a disk in you. It's not everyday a man sees a Vela outside a compound—not unless it's a dead Vela. I'd also like to know what Zone you are supposed to be in."

She shuddered. She knew he was right. No Vela were allowed to leave a Compound. To do so was to die. The disks would make certain of that.

"It's a long story," she said.

"Figured it was," he said. "We'll talk about it later. Right now sit real still and don't say another word."

He had only glanced at her occasionally as they talked because he kept watching the country around them.

She sat very still, not knowing what to expect. She knew her chances of survival were almost non-existent. Vela just were not allowed to leave a Compound and live to tell about it.

She heard the drum of hooves and felt every muscle and nerve tighten. It sounded like it was still some distance away, but she sat perfectly still. Only the Rasset were allowed to have bairan, the small, swift three-eyed horses once used by everyone. After what seemed like hours, the sound faded off into the distance.

"They won't be back for awhile," he said as he turned to look at her.

"What makes you so certain?" she asked.

"They were headed for the shore. They don't have any reason to look inland—yet. Come on, we have to start moving again."

She rose without letting the groan escape her lips. She was determined not to let him know how exhausted she was already.

He watched her get up and knew she was in a lot of pain. "It won't be long before we can rest for the night."

"Where are we going?" she asked as they began walking again.

"To a safe place," was all he said as he led off again.

She had no idea where they were going, but shortly after leaving the canyon, they entered a field where the coarse grass was taller than they were. She felt safer then, knowing that any movement they made would not be easily noticed due to the wind constantly moving the grass. Hans seemed to be following some sort of a trail, but it was not one she ever would have noticed had she been alone.

After another two hours of walking they stopped again. He handed her a canteen and said, "I'll be back in just a few minutes," and moved through the grass.

He was soon lost to sight, but she was too tired to try to follow him even if she had wanted to. All she really wanted was to lie down and sleep forever.

When Hans returned he handed her a staff.

"It'll make it a little easier for you."

They started on again. They were steadily climbing up an incline and soon came out of the tall grass. Hans stopped for just a moment to allow her to catch her breath and then turned from the fairly straight course they had been traveling.

She had noticed the sun was getting low in the sky and was relieved when he headed toward a small opening. She was too tired to care where they stopped, as long as they stopped. Her shoulder was throbbing something terrible and the rest of her body was still sore from all the bruises.

"Go on in," he said. "I have to make certain we haven't been noticed."

She had to get on hands and knees to go through the opening, but once inside, she found herself in a good sized cavern. It was damp and cool, but she noticed a fire pit and sat down close to it. Every part of her body ached and her shoulder was bleeding slightly.

A short time later, Hans entered. "Not the best looking place, but it's safe. I hung a blanket inside the opening just in case anyone should happen to pass by. If they saw light from a fire they might investigate. So now we can have a small one."

After he had started a fire, he moved to the back of the cavern and returned with another canteen filled with water.

"Drink as much as you want," he said. "There's plenty and you need to replenish your liquids."

He came toward her and she backed away.

"I need to look at that shoulder," he explained.

"It's all right," she lied.

"Then let me see it," he insisted.

She sat down and loosened the neck of her covering to allow him to see where the disk had been.

"How did you take it out?" she asked. "I thought there was no way to remove them."

"That's what they want everyone to think," he said as he removed the bandage and began to wash the area where the disk had been.

"It looks pretty good," he told her as he applied some salve and a new bandage. "We'll rest here for a day before we head out."

"You don't think they will find us?"

"Not right away. They will be looking for the Runner for a day or two. Then they will begin a more thorough search. Sorry I couldn't slow the pace down a little for you, but it was important for us to get as far from the shore as possible. I would have preferred allowing you to rest and heal first, but that would have only increased the danger."

"You seem to know a lot about what they will do," she said.

"Comes from watching them," he replied. "Watching, listening, and learning."

She desperately wanted to stay awake and find out more about this stranger, but her body was too drained. The past two days had used up all the energy she had. She was exhausted.

He pointed to a small pile of long-needled branches just a short distance from the fire and handed her two blankets. "That's your bed. You better go lie down for awhile."

She opened her mouth to protest but just couldn't force the words out—she was that tired. She crawled over, put one blanket on the branches and pulled the other one over her. When she put her head down she was asleep almost instantly.

* * *

Once again she awoke to the sound of Hans moving around the cavern. She lay there for a few moments just watching him.

She had noticed the day before that he always seemed to know exactly what to do next. There was no wasted motion in his movements.

Now she saw the same thing. He never moved unless there was a purpose, and he never seemed unsure of what to do or how to do it.

"Good afternoon." he said without turning around to look at her.

"How did you know I was awake?" she asked.

"I felt you watching me," was the response as he turned from looking out the entrance of their new residence. "Funny how you can tell when someone looks at you for more than a minute or two."

"Is it really afternoon?" she asked.

"Yes, it is. I didn't wake you sooner because we're safe enough for now and I figured you needed all the rest you could get."

"I was just wondering," she began, "how it was that you found me and why you bothered to help me."

"Well, I found you because I was watching the shore. As for why I helped you, you certainly looked like you could use a little help," was his reply. "How did you come to be washed up on the beach like that?"

She didn't know where to begin—or how much she dared tell him.

"Seems to me," he continued, "that a runaway like you should have headed inland. There are not many hiding places along the shore."

"Why do you say I'm a runaway?"

"I took the disc out—remember? The Rasset never let one of the Vela leave their Compounds."

"So you're an expert on Rasset are you?" she asked suspiciously.

"Nope. Like I said, I am just a man who's done a lot of listening and have studied them for quite some time now."

He came over to the fire pit, spooned some hot soup into a crude bowl and handed it to her. "Want to talk about it?" he asked.

"Not right now," she responded, "I don't even want to think about the past few days."

"It would help me if I had at least a little information," he continued. "I am assuming the Runner I sent out to sea was looking for you."

"I've been thinking about that." she said. "If you harmed one of the Runners they will know exactly where to look."

"Not exactly," he assured her. "By the time they find him, he will be a long way from where I blasted him."

"You what?" she asked. "You can't blast a Runner. If anything happens to one of them the Rasset know exactly where he is right away."

"Not if you disable his sash first," Hans replied. "They don't keep it turned on all the time you know. They're just able to activate it really fast. That Runner didn't know what hit him."

"How did you do it?" she asked. "I've always been told you can't hit a Runner with usual weapons."

"Well," he grinned, "that's another misconception they want you to believe. Runners are tough critters, I'll give them that. They stand up real good to most attacks, but their necks are soft. A sharp knife and it's all over. But I didn't kill him. Like you said, if I had, they would have known right away."

"How did you get close enough to him without being blasted by his stunner first?"

"My shot was intended to not only disable the transmission sash, but also to knock the Runner out—it worked."

"I still want to know how you knocked out a Runner."

"With this," he said as he pulled the glove out of the pocket in his covering.

"And what, may I ask, is that?"

"A little creation of a good friend of mine," he answered. "Packs a real punch. The only trouble is the recharge time. He's still working on reducing that."

She was amazed. *Who was this man anyway?*

"Now it's my turn," he said. "The sooner you fill me in on what started this chain of events, the sooner I'll be able to figure out what we need to do next."

"Don't I have any say in what we do?" she asked irately. "Remember, I didn't *ask* you to get involved."

"Nope. You sure didn't. And if I hadn't gotten involved, the Runner probably would have kept searching until he spotted you and transmitted your exact location to the Rasset."

"Okay, I guess I do need to thank you," she said calming down somewhat, "but I want a say in what we do next. After all, this all started because of me."

"Which brings us back to my question," he insisted. "What did you do to cause the Rasset to send a Runner to find you?"

She wanted to trust him. She *needed* to trust someone. But who could you really trust anymore? Ever since the Treaty the Merene had not been able to trust anyone. And she was not only a Merene; she was a Vela—a Vela chosen to become a Redere.

"How safe are we here?" she asked.

"That depends on how badly they want to find you. If they think you're dead, then they won't look for long, but since they have not found your body they will probably assume you are still alive."

"And that means what?" she asked.

"That means we will need to move soon."

"And just where are we going to go?" she wanted to know.

"To a safe place," was all he replied.

"Where is that now that the Treaty has withstood the test?"

"There are always safe places," he assured her. "They're just not advertised or they wouldn't be safe places."

"All right," she sighed, "my name is Arabella and I think they will not give up looking for me quickly."

"Then forget about that day of rest I mentioned. We need to get even further away as fast as we can. So you have the remainder of today and all night to rest up. We will leave at first light because we need to get out of this Zone entirely."

With that said, he got to his feet and headed toward the opening.

"Eat as much as you can and rest. I will be back after sunset,"

Arabella looked at him and felt fear creeping into the very core of her being.

"Don't worry," he said, again seeming to be reading her mind, "you are safe enough here and I will be back. I simply need to look around and scout the trail ahead."

For some strange reason she felt reassured. She was surprised at how Hans had just accepted what she told him and did not seem overly worried about anything. Yet she knew the danger he would take by leaving the Zone he was supposed to remain in. For a brief moment she thought *maybe he will just leave during the night or maybe he will simply turn me over to the Rasset* but somehow she just felt he would do neither. Something about him caused her to trust this stranger.

CHAPTER THREE

At dawn they were moving once again. When Hans had returned the night before, he had modified her moccasins to fit better. Now he gave her three food packets and a canteen. He would have preferred traveling at night, but ever since the Demonstration the terrain had been changed too much and there were too many places that looked solid enough, but were, in reality, just thin coverings over deep pits.

He allowed his mind to replay the scene he had witnessed less than a year ago. He had just begun scouting out some safe places where the New Confederates could hide or store supplies.

He had heard the Rasset were planning a Demonstration to convince the people there was no point in resisting them. As he had been looking over the familiar landscape, a bright light had suddenly shot through the air and illuminated a large area. Although there was no sound, he felt the ground begin to shake and he watched in amazement as the land began to seemingly melt right before his eyes. What had been a valley was suddenly a canyon and holes, like Swiss cheese, appeared wherever the bright light had touched. He had been glad he had decided to look the valley over before going any further or he would have been over his head in water. What had once been a river was widened into a sea twenty miles or more across. The New Confederates had named it the Middle Sea.

He learned later that there had been several such areas that the Rasset had apparently chosen to divide the country and convince the people of the futility of resistance. The other areas were not changed as drastically but each one became a treacherous death trap full of deep pits hidden by seemingly solid ground. Those foolish enough to attempt crossing one of these areas risked falling to their death. The Merene began referring to these areas as Separations. Not long after the Demonstration, the leaders of the Resistance had agreed to the treaty the Rasset offered.

The Rasset had quickly set up headquarters, establishing a Compound in each of the Zones. No one knew why they chose certain people to be set apart from the rest of the population, but those they chose were not allowed to leave the Compound to which they were assigned. Later it was learned that a small metal disk was implanted on the back of their left shoulder to insure that if any did leave they could be tracked, or "disposed of", immediately.

At first there had been a protest from the heads of the Resistance, but the Rasset quickly pointed out that the Treaty allowed them to keep a certain number of Merene in Compounds to ensure no one would try to break the terms of the Treaty. That was when everyone was classified either Vela or Reth. Hans was glad Diwesh were considered Reth.

Hans stopped so suddenly Arabella almost walked into him. They had been following a game trail among the rocks and were now about to enter what seemed to be a meadow. She watched as he surveyed the open area in front of them. His eyes quickly scanned the landscape, and then he began a much more careful study of the perimeter. Only after he was satisfied there was nothing there, did he whisper for her to follow exactly in his footsteps, and he began to slowly walk across the open field.

Who is this man and why is he helping me? she wondered again.

He motioned for her to follow as he stooped down and moved slowly to their right. It seemed to take forever because they would take a few steps; stop and wait, then take a few more steps.

Just when she thought her back and legs would be forever stuck in this uncomfortable position, he stepped into the brush surrounding the meadow. After a few more steps, he indicated she was to go into a small opening. Like before, she had to almost crawl on hands and knees but after only a short distance, she once again found herself in a large room.

He came in right behind her, placed a weaving of twigs over the small opening, and moved to the fire pit in the middle of the room. In moments he had a small flame going. She watched as he went to the back of the room. For the first time she had a chance to really look at this man. He was not a big man, but somehow he instilled a confidence in his ability to handle whatever difficulties they might encounter. He had shoulder length blonde hair and a brown beard. She could imagine him sitting in one of the longboats that had sailed the Eastern Sea for exploration and trade many years ago. Her thoughts were interrupted when Hans returned wearing a blue covering and carrying another one of the same color and two small packets of salted meat. He began heating the meat over the fire and said, "Better put that on. It's the correct color for this Zone."

"You mean we just crossed a Separation?" she asked incredulously.

"That's right. Two more days like today and we'll be there," he said.

"And just where is 'there'?" she asked.

"The home of a few friends of mine in this Zone."

"And what happens to me then?"

"That all depends on you," he replied. "Are you going to tell me how you managed to escape and what your plans are?"

She took a deep breath. "Well, as you have guessed I was one of the Vela," she began.

"Reason you had the disk implant," he commented.

"Yes. I've been in Compound Five for about six months now."

"That's the first Compound they set up on the western side of the Middle Sea."

"Right. It's in the south of what used to be Nordum."

"So how did you wind up here, east of the Middle Sea?"

"I was being transported to another location."

"I thought that wasn't allowed."

"Technically it isn't. But the Rasset aren't as honorable as they like to have people think they are."

"Aren't the Resistance people still doing monthly inventories of who is in each Compound?"

"Yes, but the inspectors are not allowed to talk to the Vela. They have to go by bracelets the Rasset put on each one."

"So as long as the head count is right, no one knows if the bracelet is on the right body?"

"Right. So when they want to move some of us, they do it one or two at a time. Only the Rasset know who's who and they rely on the disks for that."

"Which brings up a subject in which I am very interested—how did your disk get damaged? We haven't been able to open one, let alone damage it."

"I wish I could tell you. All I remember is hearing something behind me and when I turned I felt a terrific blow to my shoulder. That was the last I remember until I woke up in your cave."

"So you have no idea how you got on the beach?"
"None at all. I wish I did."

* * *

At dawn the next day they were up and moving again. Arabella was able to travel somewhat faster and Hans picked up the pace slightly. They walked all day taking only three short rest periods at locations Hans chose because they allowed him to survey the surrounding country. He didn't seem inclined to talk much, being preoccupied with watching and listening. It was after sunset when they finally came to another cave. This time he prepared some sort of stew. Arabella wasn't sure what was in it but she was so tired and hungry that any hot food would have tasted good. When Hans returned from rinsing out the wooden bowls he found her fast asleep. Looking at her, he wondered what was going to happen. He had never heard of anyone escaping from one of the Compounds and living to tell of it. Arabella may be the very first and there were several people who would want to question her. He had a few questions of his own but they could wait. The most important thing right now was getting her to safety.

* * *

As the sky was starting to turn pink with the morning sun, Hans woke Arabella and handed her a refilled canteen and two more food packets. He was glad he had stored several cases of them in various locations for just such an emergency. The packets would last indefinitely and provided the needed nourishment even if they did lack much flavor.

"Think you can take one more day of travel?" he asked.

"You set the pace and I'll keep up," she replied defiantly.

Hans grinned. He knew that few people could keep up for long with the pace at which he usually traveled, but her reply showed spunk.

As they started out Arabella thought about how much the landscape had changed. There were fewer hills and trees and more open areas and tall grass. Hans avoided the open areas as much as possible and never crossed one without first spending time surveying the area carefully.

Today he did not stop for a midday rest. Arabella did not question him; she had made up her mind to trust this man—at least for the time being. She knew all too well that if the Rasset found her they would either kill her or take her back to one of the Compounds. She shuddered at the very thought of it. She would not return there. She could not allow them to take her alive.

Once more Hans stopped suddenly. Taking a small, flute-like object from the pocket of his covering he blew three soft notes. A few moments later Arabella heard a similar three notes from somewhere ahead. Then Hans blew two more soft notes. If she had not seen the flute herself, Arabella would have thought it was the sound of birds.

"Let's go. But walk slowly and quietly," he instructed her.

"Are we there then?" she asked.

"Almost. When we do get there let me do the talking—and don't worry—even though they look a little rough they are good people."

What did he mean by that? she wondered.

Hans walked over to a small shack that was built against the hillside. He went toward the back wall and disappeared. Arabella walked to where she had last seen him and suddenly felt a cool breeze. Turning at a right angle to face the breeze she saw Hans standing in a dark passageway.

Taking her by the arm, Hans led the way into the passage and picked up a torch, lit it and handed it to Arabella. Taking another for himself, he led off into the darkness. The light only illuminated a short distance, but they began walking into the cool, damp darkness ahead of them. After a few minutes Arabella could tell they were going downhill. After traveling a short distance, Hans stood still and held out his arm to stop her. Looking past him to where he was pointing she saw a huge pit right in front of them.

"Didn't want you to bump into me and make me lose my balance."

"I can understand that," she replied. "How deep is that pit?"

"Don't know. Nature formed it a long time ago and didn't bother to provide an easy way down."

Flattening himself against the cavern wall, Hans moved sideways along a very narrow ledge on one side of the pit. Nervously, Arabella followed, the toes of her moccasins hanging over the edge as she pressed her back against the cold wall.

After going about a third of the way around the pit, they came to a natural corridor. Hans moved more rapidly now and Arabella still had the feeling they were going downhill and was certain it was getting colder. She had to trust he knew the way because she could not see much by the dim light, and they were moving too fast for her to see details anyway. Occasionally she heard the sound of small creatures and tried not to think about some of the animals who inhabited cool, dark places.

The passage took a sharp turn and became slightly brighter. Soon, Hans stopped at an arched opening and extinguished the torch before placing it in a box which held several other torches.

"I know it hasn't been a very easy trip for you, and I appreciate the fact that you didn't whine or complain at all," he said as he turned to look at her. "You will be safe here and we will have some time to figure out what to do next."

"Just where is 'here'?" she asked. "And who are 'we'?"

"We're in one of the Undergrounds and 'we' are some of the New Confederates."

"*One* of the Undergrounds? You mean there are more of these? And who are the New Confederates?"

"The New Confederates are men and women—both Merene and Reth—who are determined to stop the Rasset and make this a free country once again. I'll explain more later. Right now let's get you introduced to a few people who may become very important to you—you are already very important to them."

With that he led the way through the archway and into a warm, illuminated corridor. Here the walls were not natural stone like the ones in the passage they had been traveling. They were made out of some kind of plaster. About waist high there was a band of material that gave off some degree of heat and light.

Arabella had no idea what lay ahead, but for the first time in over a year, she did feel the Rasset could not find her easily. It felt like a tremendous burden had been lifted from her shoulders.

A few minutes later they came to a set of doors. Hans took a strangely shaped object from his pocket and inserted one end of it into a small opening in the door. Immediately the door swung open and he took her by the wrist and pulled her through.

"Don't mean to be rough," he apologized, "but it only stays open for a few moments. I've kind of gotten used to you and didn't want to see you crushed when it swung shut."

"Thanks—I think. Does that mean I am a prisoner here now?"

"Not at all, but you will need an escort to lead you out."

"Then I am practically a prisoner," she said.

"Don't compare our security to their tyranny. Ours is simply for self-preservation. If, after learning a little more about us, you desire to leave, no one will stop you. You are free—or at least as free as any of us are with the Rasset around—and you may make your own decisions and choices.

But before you make those decisions, I want you to come with me and meet those people I mentioned to you."

With that he headed down the corridor. After going only a short distance, they came to a door on one side of the corridor. Hans reached up to a stone about shoulder height above the floor and pushed on it. The door swung open revealing a large room containing a square table with benches on every side of it.

"Help yourself to some water," he said, indicating a small hole with water running out of it and into a stone sink. "I'll be back in less than fifteen minutes."

With that he left the room and Arabella was totally alone for the first time since she had been chosen to be one of the Vela.

She walked over to a shelf above the sink and found a cup. Taking a small amount of water she tested it and found that it was truly refreshing—not brackish like the water in the canteen. She had not realized just how thirsty she was and quickly filled the cup. Then she began a careful study of her surroundings. The room was really nothing more than a cavern with a door closing off the narrow natural opening. About halfway up the walls was a band of the same material she had noticed in the corridors after passing through the first set of doors. There was an oval of what appeared to be the same material on the ceiling. Between the band around the room and the oval in the ceiling, the room was quite well lit and comfortable. Holding her hand near the band she discovered that it did, in fact, give off some heat, but was not hot.

For the first time in a long time, Arabella began to think about the situation she was in. She knew nothing about Hans and his friends and was afraid of being found by the Rasset. What did the future hold for her?

CHAPTER FOUR

Hans returned with three other men. They each took a seat on one of the benches and Hans motioned Arabella to sit down. Then he introduced each of them.

"Arabella, this is Hazcra, Hanta, and Haisa."

Hazcra was slender but muscular, with a mass of thick black hair and a quick grin that lit up his whole face. There was a small scar on his left cheek. Hanta was very muscular with curly blond hair, perfect white teeth, and a constant smile. His arms were well muscled and attached to a huge chest. Haisa was the tallest of the three and also obviously muscular with straight blond hair and an expressionless face. Unlike the other two, he never seemed to smile at all.

"Arabella," Hans said as he sat down himself, "I haven't asked you a lot of questions for two reasons. One, I thought you needed a little time to adjust to your situation and two, I wanted these men to hear, first-hand, anything you can tell us."

"Just who are you and what is this all about?" she asked.

"As I told you, we are one part of the New Confederacy, a group that is dedicated to breaking the hold the Rasset have on everyone, including the Resistance," Hans replied, "and you are a very important person as far as we are concerned. To our knowledge no one has ever escaped from a Compound and no one has ever had a disk implant and lived to tell about it."

"Well, I don't know what it is you think I can tell you."

"Let's start with just what your position in the Compound was," suggested the man with a thick mass of dark hair who had been introduced as Hazcra.

"As I told Hans, I was a Vela—one of those chosen to insure peace between the Resistance and the Rasset. I was being transported to another compound where I was to become a Redere."

She noticed Hans raised one eyebrow at this.

"So what happened?" asked Hanta, the most muscular of the three newcomers.

Arabella looked into his eyes and noticed they were also two different colors, in fact, all four of the men in the room had that uniquely Diwesh trait.

"I wish I knew," she replied. "Like I told Hans, all I remember is hearing something behind me and when I started to turn I felt a terrific blow to my shoulder and that was the last thing I remember until I woke up in his cave."

"How were you being transported?" asked Haisa, the tallest of them all.

"In a sky sled. There were three other girls in it already when it landed in Compound Five. Two Rasset and two Dura were there also, one in front, one in the back and one on each side of the sled."

"How long after you got into the sled before you were struck?" asked Hanta.

"Maybe two hours."

"Hmm. A sky sled with eight passengers traveling about two hours..." Haisa spoke as if to himself. He seemed to be doing some mental calculations.

"Was there any talking? Did anyone say anything that would give you an idea where they were taking you," asked Hans.

"One of the other girls had just started to say something to me about not wanting to be a Redere."

"Did the Rasset hear her?"

"I don't think so. She spoke very quietly and the noise of the wings of the neox probably drowned out her voice. The only reason I could hear her was because she was standing right next to me."

"I imagine it was pretty cramped," said Hazcra, "there's not much room in those sky sleds. Especially for that many people. The usual load is four. Six is crowded. Eight would really be cramped."

"Do you have any idea at all why there were so many passengers?" Hans asked.

"I did hear one of them say they had to hurry and get back because there was an inspection due tomorrow."

"The girl who spoke to you," Hanta asked, "what did she look like? Did she give you a name? Do you have any idea what Compound she was from?"

"She had dark hair—almost black—and a small mole on her right cheek. I have no idea what her name was as we had not dared talk until then. As for what Compound she was from, I have no idea but the color of her covering was black."

"That helps us a lot." Hans said. "What color were the coverings of the other girls."

"I hadn't thought about it before, but they were all different. Hers was black, one was yellow, and the other one was red."

"Why did they have three from the other side of the country?" Hanta said to Hans."

"I'm almost afraid to find out," he replied. "To our knowledge they've never transported Vela across the Middle Sea before"

"Was there any noise just before you felt that blow from behind?" Haisa suddenly interrupted.

"No noise. In fact the sound of the wings of the neox suddenly grew quieter now that I think about it."

"Were you going up or down in altitude?"

"I think we were going up. Why?"

"You think you know what happened Haisa?" Hans asked.

"I have a theory that I am fairly certain will prove to be correct. Neox are pretty dependable as work birds but they have one flaw. If a load is too heavy for them, they don't stop or slow down at all. They just keep on going until they pass out or die from the strain. I'm guessing that the sudden blow Arabella felt was the body of the neox. Those foolish Rasset overloaded the sky sled. They probably would have been okay if they had allowed the neox to rest for an hour or so. But if they had been flying for any length of time before they picked her up and then went two hours more, they could have very easily pushed the neox to the limit. Even under the best of conditions eight passengers for over two hours is a lot for one of those work birds. If they were climbing when he passed out he would have fallen back toward the sky sled, and if Arabella was standing up she could have been knocked right out of the sled."

"What would have happened to the others then?" Hazcra asked.

"Depends on how high they were and where they landed. Since Hans found Arabella washed ashore I am assuming they were crossing the Middle Sea. The other seven may have also washed ashore but since they weren't knocked out of the sled they may have chosen to stay with it. If the other neox were falling, and pulling the sled behind him, they would have fallen faster due to all the weight. My guess is that they either drowned or crashed."

"That would explain why I saw several groups of searchers before we left the Brown Zone," Hans stated. "The Rasset do not like to lose track of any of their own and if there were four Redere as well, they would not have wasted any time trying to locate them. If Haisa is right and they were headed east, it's a good thing we headed north."

"So what do you think damaged the disc?" Hanta asked.

"Well," Haisa began, "either she hit the water with that shoulder or—and I think this is more likely—the beak of the Neox hit it. The beak of a falling neox could pack quite a wallop."

"If she fell into the Middle Sea and was washed ashore at high tide, it would explain all her scrapes and bruises. That shoreline is full of rocks and broken seashells," Hans interjected.

"Well, we don't have any facts, but it certainly does sound like a logical theory," Hanta stated.

"It'll do until we hear a better one," Hans stated. "Haisa, why don't you get started analyzing the disk; Hanta, set up a meeting with the representatives from each of the Zones for tomorrow afternoon. Something is going on and we need to find out what it is and prepare to try to disrupt it. Hazcra, take Arabella to meet your wife and set up a place for her to sleep. I'm certain she could use some rest. She's still weak and she's been trying to keep up with my pace for the past five days."

"'Nuff said," Hazcra replied as he got up from his seat and waited for Arabella to stand up.

She looked at Hans, but he was already on his way out the door along with the other two. Too tired to protest, Arabella followed Hazcra down the corridor to a stairway and down the stairs to another corridor which they traveled until they came to stop in front of a door that opened when he touched a stone in the wall.

When they entered she noticed this chamber was quite a bit different from the one they had just left. Although it had a band of the same material she saw everywhere that seemed to provide light and warmth, there was a more subdued light here and, unlike the other room, it had been decorated with curtains and draperies and there were rugs on the floor.

As soon as they entered, a woman with short dark hair came from behind one of the draperies.

"Acir, this is Arabella. A stray Hans picked up and brought here."

"A stray?" Acir asked, a questioning look in her dark eyes.

"Long story, honey, but I'll fill you in over some dinner. I don't imagine Hans has cooked up any meals that could begin to compare to mine. You know how he seems to exist on those food pouches."

"All right. While you throw something together I'll fix up a place for her to sleep tonight but I had better be told all about it at dinner."

"That's a promise. While you're doing that, Arabella can set back and relax."

With that Arabella found herself alone again. What kind of place was this and what was going to happen to her?

* * *

Hazcra did fill Acir in while the three of them ate dinner and, as Arabella listened to his relating of events, for the first time in almost a year she began to feel safe and at peace.

She watched his facial expressions and listened as he gave an accurate account to their brief meeting. He seemed to be one of those natural born story tellers. An individual who could take even a dull situation or topic and make it come alive by the way he told it. She was surprised to find herself even laughing when he painted a vivid picture of an overworked neox struggling to pull a sky sled and suddenly falling back and knocking her out of the sled in the process. It had been a very long time since she had laughed at anything.

"Well," Acir said when her husband was finished, "looks like we have another Confederate, or do you want to go back to the Rasset?"

"No, I do *not* want to go back," Arabella replied emphatically. "However, I would like to know a little more about this 'New Confederate' group before I just jump into the frying pan."

"That's a real good idea," Hazcra said, "as long as you understand we cannot tell you too much until we're certain you want to be one of us. The Rasset would love to know more about us. So far we have been able to keep a pretty low profile while still disrupting some of their plans."

"That's right," Acir added, "our closest call came about two years ago and we do not want a repeat of that."

"No we don't," Hazcra stated. "We almost lost Hans and we did lose one of our undergrounds. So we are more cautious now. In fact, I was surprised that Hans brought you here, until he told me about taking the disk out of your shoulder. Then I understood. He didn't feel he had any choice except to bring you here for your own safety.

"So let me give you a quick outline about us and our organization. We call ourselves the New Confederates because that is the type of government we hope to be able to establish when we rid ourselves of the Rasset. Our goal is to remove the Rasset and set up a confederacy of the Zones. Each Zone would be part of an overall group where they would be represented. The Headquarters would work together to protect and benefit each of the Zones, but each Zone would be independent and the representatives would be accountable to the people in their area. They would live and work in their Zone and would meet at the Headquarters on a regular basis. There would be no such thing as a career politician or a government that could tax or create laws for any Zone. Each Zone would make their own laws and levy their own taxes to be used in their part of the confederacy. The Headquarters would be for protection and Zone cooperation and improvements only. The mess we are in now is the result of a big central government and career politicians who thought they were above the laws they passed and the taxes they imposed on everyone else but they were exempted. Our goal is to prevent such a tragedy from ever happening again."

"But I thought the Resistance was protecting us from the Rasset. Aren't the Inspectors Resistance officials?"

"The Resistance only gives the impression that they are protecting us from the Rasset. In reality they are powerless to do much. You see, the Rasset are actually former government officials."

"That can't be true! When the Rasset attacked us the Resistance was formed by our former government leaders. They worked out a peace arrangement with the Rasset."

"Some peace arrangement! An agreement that keeps some of our people in Compounds as little more than slaves."

"You claim the Rasset are really our former government officials. Then who are the Resistance leaders?"

"When the Rasset decided to take control of the country they wanted everyone to believe, like you did, that it was an outside group. If people had been aware that it was their own government officials, there would have been much more resistance. By doing it the way they did and pretending they defeated our military, there was little time to organize any real opposition. How could our military fight an enemy that included most of the top military leaders?"

"I can see where that would be difficult."

"The Rasset reached a point where they got tired of putting up the front that they were working for, or representing, the people. They felt they knew what was best for everyone and decided to impose their ideas on the very ones who had put them in power. The Resistance is made up of government officials who were not part of the upper level coalition or those few who actually tried to serve the people."

"If the Rasset are really former government leaders why did they set up the Compounds?" she asked.

"The Compounds serve two purposes. First, they reassure the people that the Resistance is protecting us from what would otherwise be a takeover by a foreign power. Secondly, by holding a certain percentage of our population hostage—because that is what the Vela really are—they hope to prevent any uprising. Who wants to attack a Compound that is filled with their fellow citizens?"

"What you are saying sounds ridiculous but I suppose it could be possible," Arabella stated. "I can attest to the hostage aspect, but what can anyone do about it if it is true?"

"That's where the New Confederates come in. So far we have only been a nuisance to the Rasset. Upsetting some of their plans and forcing them to move slowly to keep up the façade. However, they are beginning to make some very big, very dangerous, changes and you—whether you know it or not—were a key piece in their plans."

"What do you mean? What do I have to do with all this?"

"You said you were being transported to another Compound to become a Redere. Do you know what the Redere are?"

"Not really. I thought it was some sort of a selected group and hoped I would find my life was going to get easier."

"You were right on both counts. It is a selected group and you would have been delivered from the slave labor the Rasset use the Vela for, but did you ever wonder why all the Redere are females? We believe you were part of the first group being taken to the Rasset's newest Compound where they plan to impregnate Redere. The offspring are to be used for—hold onto your supper—food!"

"Now I *know* you are wrong. Even the Rasset are not cannibals."

"Are you sure? You see as the years have gone by the Rasset have continued to look for new excitement and pleasures. It began with fancy government dinners and resorts, but each year it needed to be bigger and better than the year before. Several years ago—shortly before the Rasset made their move, several of our government officials attended a dinner where human baby was the main course. I know it sounds impossible, but remember they actually believed they were above the law and above society's standards of right and wrong. Like so many other new and novel things it created a desire for more, and since simply killing babies outright would not be tolerated by the masses, they have been using aborted babies for several years now, but the new delicacy is the flesh of a two year old child. There is more meat per child and it is claimed to still be tender."

"Hazcra", Acir interrupted, "I think this poor girl needs some time to rest and to think about all this. Arabella, let me show you to your room for tonight."

"Thank you. I really do need time to rest and think. All of this is overwhelming."

CHAPTER FIVE

When Arabella awoke the next morning Hans was sitting at the table drinking coffee and talking with Hazcra and Acir.

As she entered the room she heard him say, "We don't know for certain, but we can't afford to take a chance."

"Then let me go with you," Hazcra replied.

"That will leave them shorthanded here and you need to finish developing the stun glove and other weapons you are working on."

"We don't want you going alone," Acir stated. "If anything happens to you the whole southern area will be unwatched. It will be bad enough to have you gone for a week. Anything longer could be disastrous. Besides, if they mount a thorough search for Arabella they will probably start in that Zone."

"I thought about that last night," Hans stated, "and I don't think they will be looking there. From what Arabella told us they were further north. I think she was carried downstream for quite a ways before she washed ashore. It's really a wonder she didn't drown."

"Mind if I join in?" Arabella said as she made her presence known.

"Not at all, in fact you might be able to help us out," Hazcra said. "You said you were the last one to be picked up?"

"That's right. After I was escorted to the sky sled the Dura entered it and we took off."

"So from Compound Number Five you headed south?"

"I don't think it was due south. It seemed a little east as well."

"Then it does fit with what I suspected," Hans stated. "I'm willing to wager fifteen food pouches they were headed for Mystery Island."

"It seems that way," Hazcra replied, "That's why we need to know more about that blasted place. All we have to go on are rumors and guesswork."

"But with what Arabella told us, it all seems to fit. I'm going to talk with Haisa and Hanta first. Then the four of us need to take it to the Council." With that he rose from the table and headed for the door.

"Wait," Arabella said, "what about me? What am I supposed to do now?"

"That depends on what you want. If you want to return to the Compound we will make arrangements to get you there, and if . . ."

"If I want to *return*?" she said with her voice rising. "Who in their right mind wants to be held in one of the Compounds?"

"Oh, so you're in your right mind now?" Hans asked with that slight smile of his. "Yesterday you didn't seem to want to leave the known behind."

"Yesterday I didn't know there were any options."

"We could use more help here," Acir stated, "that is, if she wants to stay with us 'moles'."

"That is up to her and the Council. If it is something you would like to do I can bring it up when the boys and I meet with them later today."

"I do think I would like to stay here—at least for awhile. But if I later decide I don't want to stay here will I be free to go?"

"No one is held here against their will. However, those who have not decided if they are totally in agreement with our cause have limited access to some areas and information."

"That makes sense."

"We haven't had many defectors," Hazcra said, "but even one defector can do a lot of damage. I have taken an oath that if I ever see Hepnet again he will pay dearly."

"Hazcra," Acir said with a worried look on her face, "don't go looking for him. You promised you wouldn't. He is just plain evil."

"Not as evil as that Cibth he listened to. I still think she was behind everything."

"Maybe so," Hans said, "but he did not have to go along with her. I tried to warn him. Let's not bring that whole thing up again. We have much more important work to do right now. I need to find out if Haisa has had any success analyzing the disk."

With that he went out the door and walked down the corridor until he came to a door marked "Caution—knock before entering."

* * *

"So," Acir said as she turned to face Arabella, "how would you like a guided tour of 'the Mole Hole' as we call it?"

"I'd love it." She replied. "If this might be my new home for awhile, I need to know my way around."

"It's not hard," Hazcra stated. "There are three levels and they are laid out quite simply with one main room at the center of each level. The center room is surrounded by a corridor which has eight corridors leading away from it. You entered on the first level and if you had gone just a little further down the corridor you would have come to the Meeting Room. It's sort of a community center where we spend much of our free time. You might run into anyone who's connected with the New Confederates there. The rest of the level is made up of meeting rooms and troop quarters. Anyone on duty stays on that level for their appointed watch. Only those on that level are required to wear the Rasset mandated coverings in case they need to go outside in a hurry. The second level, the one you're on now, has the Supply Room at the center. That is where we get any of the supplies we need. Everything from food and clothing to medical supplies are kept there. The remainder of this level is made up of living quarters and storage. The lowest level has the Council Room at the center. The rest is research rooms, weapon storage, and other military needs. You will only be allowed on the third level if called for and then you will be escorted by at least two New Confederates."

"I had no idea there was any resistance to the Rasset after the treaty was signed."

"That's the way we want it." Hanta stated as he joined the conversation. Arabella had not even heard him enter. Just like Hans, all three of the new men she had met seemed to be able to walk soundlessly.

"If they don't feel threatened they are more likely to be lax in their defense, which brings me to a point I would like to talk to you about. How much can you tell us about the operations and fortifications of the Compounds?"

"Not as much as I think you would like to know, I'm afraid."

"Anything you can tell us will help." Hanta replied.

"Well, I've only been in two of the Compounds but they were almost identical as far as I could tell. As you probably have seen, each Compound is a perfect square with the Vela quarters in the center. There is a gate in the center of the east and west walls. On each corner is a tower which looks out over the surrounding area. I don't know how far they can see from the towers but they always have two Dura in each one."

"Are they connected in any way on the inside of the wall? I mean is there any kind of a raised walkway connecting them for soldier movement?"

"No, each one has an entrance door at ground level."

"Then how is the wall protected in case of attack?"

"There is a ground walkway around the entire perimeter that is kept clear at all times. If there were an attack, Dura could get there quickly and there are holes to shoot arrows through. They also have crossbows."

"Thanks," Hanta replied, "that actually helps us quite a bit."

"I wish I could tell you more."

"Just talk to us about your life in the Compound," Hazcra said, "that will reveal more to us than you might think."

"But first," Acir interrupted, "we have a tour to go on."

"I'll leave that to the two of you," Hanta said as he headed for the door. "I'm not much of a tour guide and there are a few things I need to take care of before the meeting with the Zone representatives and the Council. Make sure you're there on time Hazcra. You know how Hans hates for any of us to be late."

"I'll be there. Acir will make certain of that."

* * *

As they began moving down the corridor Arabella found herself truly drawn to this couple. The three of them went back up to the first level and the Meeting Room. It was a large, round room with four doors into it. The ceiling was almost totally made up of the same strange material as the band she had seen in every corridor and room. The light from it illuminated the whole room almost as brightly as the sun outside. All the walls had been covered with a plaster of some sort to give them a smooth surface.

The room was full of people sitting at tables, talking or playing some sort of card game. Arabella was introduced to several people including a rather round, jovial woman named Yamam who smiled a lot. She was also introduced to a man named Neliv who was dark skinned, seemed to have been hewn out of the very rock of the mountains, and looked about as old. Everyone she met seemed pleasant and genuinely interested in making her feel welcome.

Next, she was taken back down to the second level and the Supply Room which was the same size and shape as the Meeting Room and had the same material on the ceiling which provided the same bright lighting. She was amazed at the variety and amount of things kept there. Anything anyone could need in the way of food or clothing was available. There were countless cases of food pouches as well as cooking equipment, coverings, and moccasins.

After leaving the Supply Room, they headed down one of the eight corridors that branched off the one surrounding the Supply Room. She noticed that the top of the band of strange material that ran down every corridor and was in every room was a different color in each corridor.

"Each door in these corridors is the entrance to a different dwelling unit," Acir said. "We'd like you to meet one more person. Probably one of the sweetest people you will ever meet." With that she touched a stone and a door opened.

As they entered the room Acir called out, "Areboh, I'd like you to meet someone else who needs to spend some time with you."

"Come on in and sit down." A lady with gray streaks in her dark hair invited as she came from an adjoining room. She led the way to a cozy kitchen area with a large table and several chairs. One was occupied by a young woman with long, straight, blonde hair and dual colored eyes and in another there was what looked like an older version of the same young woman.

"Areboh, I imagine Hans has told you about Arabella already, "Acir stated, "but I thought you would like to meet her yourself."

"Of course she would and so would we," said the first young woman. "I'm Ahe, Hazcra's sister—although I don't admit that to everyone" she said with a big smile on her lips.

Arabella could see a family resemblance.

"And I am Accebe, also Hazcra's sister. He is my 'little' brother."

"And Areboh is our mother," Hazcra added as he helped himself to some koieos, a sweet snack, that was piled on a plate in the middle of the table.

"So, you are the young lady Hans found," Areboh stated. "I was hoping to be able to meet you soon. Please have a seat."

"Arabella," Acir said as she sat down herself, "Areboh is the adopted mother of many of the New Confederates. Anyone who needs a listening ear, a hug, or a meal, finds their way to Areboh's home. That's why I wanted to introduce you to her. I thought you might be in need of a 'mother' while you sort things out."

"Well, I know when it's time to make an exit," Hazcra stated. "When you have five women wanting to talk it is no place for a man. Besides, I need to head for the meeting." With that he got up and headed for the door.

* * *

After knocking on the door marked "Caution" Hans heard a "Come in" and entered a room filled with eight slate tables all cluttered with laboratory equipment. Haisa stood at one table on the right hand side. He was bent over some strange looking equipment and seemed totally engrossed in what he was doing.

"Any luck?" Hans asked.

"Actually, yes," Haisa replied as he turned and picked up one of the two scuzzets that were allowed to roam around the room. Scuzzets were small, thin, animals with brown and green fur that were curious about everything and everybody. They were extremely hard to catch and train but, once trained; they were totally devoted and never strayed too far from their master. They would use their two inch long sharp teeth and razor sharp claws to attack anyone they considered a threat to their master.

"I've been up all night taking this disc apart. It appears that when it is activated remotely it does not stop the heart like we were told. It is really just a simple device that takes hydrogen from the air and fills the lungs with it. It causes the hydrogen to react with the oxygen in the lungs and the host drowns because their lungs fill with water. I can't tell for certain how quickly it works but I suspect it's pretty fast."

"So why haven't we been able to open any discs before?"

"We thought it was sealed somehow but that's not true. Once it has been activated, the disc collapses in on itself and it is actually fused together, thereby making it impossible to open."

"So, can you disrupt the signal to prevent it from working?"

"I was just finishing that. The signal has to be pretty powerful because it will reach any disc in a given Zone, but I think if someone had a blocking device fairly close to the disc, it would interrupt the signal and nullify it."

"Do you think you could make about six signal disrupters?" Hans asked with a slight grin as he picked up the other scuzzet who had just come over to satisfy its curiosity.

"Of course, I just need a little time. But I would have no way of testing them for certain. However, I am afraid the signal for each Zone might be different."

"I don't think so," Hans said. "They would want to be able to use it on a Vela who ran from one Zone to another."

"You're probably right. That will make it much easier to build some disrupters."

"As for testing them, I am afraid we'll just have to trust your theory. There is no way to try them out first."

Just then there was a knock on the door.

"Come on in," Haisa called out.

The door opened and Hanta strode in.

"Figured I'd find you here," he said to Hans. "I know you wouldn't have brought her here unless you were certain there was little risk, but I need to know more about her. After all, security around here is my responsibility."

"We all need to learn more about her, but I'm more concerned with what we can learn *from* her. We've never had an opportunity to find out about the workings of a Compound from someone who has actually been a Vela but I understand your concern. From the very first night I kept a close watch on her and all the way here I kept looking for any indication that she might be a plant. You know my observations and impressions are pretty reliable. I did not see anything to cause any concern. I think she is exactly what she seems to be—a confused, scared, young lady who, like so many other people, doesn't understand all that has happened, and whose whole world has been turned upside down."

Hanta stood there with his arms crossed over his large chest.

"I figured as much. Just wanted to hear it from you."

"You know," Hans said, "since you took over as head of security you've done a great job but I hope you aren't letting your medical responsibilities suffer."

"Not to worry. There really isn't much call for my medical skills as long as security is kept up. That's why I was willing to take the position. Besides, it helps me stay on top of things that are going on around here."

"Well, you might want to talk to your brother Hazcra then. He's talking about going with me on a little trip I'm planning to make. You know how much he's needed here right now. His weapons development is vital to us."

"It sure is. That and Haisa's research are probably the most important things going right now. I'll have a talk with him. Now what's this trip you mentioned?"

"I'm going to tell the Council that I need to go to Mystery Island for about a week."

"Do you think you can do it in that amount of time?"

"I have to—that or less. If what we suspect is true, they are moving faster than we thought. They don't think there is any organized resistance—that's our advantage—but if they establish their headquarters on the island it will be much harder to pull it off."

"All right, but we better get going. The Council is meeting soon."

Haisa and Hans put down the scuzzets they were holding and the three of them were just leaving the lab when Hazcra came down the corridor. Together the four of them headed for the Council Room.

CHAPTER SIX

"So, tell us a little about yourself," Areboh stated as she filled cups with a hot drink. There was one for each of the five women. Arabella took a sip and found that it was delicious.

"There's really not much to tell. I was working on my family's farm, where we kept about thirty niso—their meat was the most tender of any niso because we were very careful what we fed them—then one day a sky sled came with two of the Resistance Inspectors and two Rasset. They informed my parents that I was to be a Vela for the sake of keeping the peace. My father started to protest and one of the Rasset talked about what an honor it would be to have one of our family play such an important part in the peace between them and the Resistance. Father still protested saying I was their only child left. My two brothers were both killed in one of the skirmishes when the Rasset took control. The Rasset said it was either I go with them or they would use the farm for one of their Compounds. The farm has been in our family for ten generations. I told my father I would go."

"How long ago did this happen?" asked Ahe.

"A little over a year ago. Right after the Demonstration."

Just then a short, dark-haired woman entered the room.

"Sorry, I did not know you had company," she said with a slight accent. "I can come back later."

"You will do no such thing," Areboh said pleasantly. "Arabella, this is Ahona, Hanta's wife. Ahona, this is Arabella. Hans found her washed up on the shore and brought her here. She was a Vela."

Ahona's eyes widened at this last statement. Taking a cup of the hot drink Areboh offered her, she sat down next to Ahe.

"What is it like living in a Compound?" Accebe asked.

"Well, for me it was not as bad as it was for some of the girls. I was appointed to be basically a maid. Every day I had to clean the living quarters of five Rasset as well as serve their meals."

"Now *that* does not sound like any fun to me," Ahe stated. "I would much rather be outside either trying to get more information about the Rasset or hunting."

"Hunting?!" Arabella exclaimed. "I did not think that was allowed."

"It's not," Ahe replied calmly. "That's why I enjoy doing it. I guess I'm as much of a rebel as the rest of my family."

"But whenever she goes outside the Underground she must dress in a dirty covering, smear mud on her face and arms, and walk with a limp," Areboh explained.

"Why?"

"So if she is noticed she will not be wanted. The Rasset do not want any who are flawed in any way."

"Besides," Ahe added, "I think it's fun to dress up and pretend to be something I am not."

"Now tell me a little about the rest of you," Arabella said.

"What would you like to know?" Accebe asked.

"Well, first of all I'd like to know a little bit about the man who brought me here. I traveled with him for five days and don't know anything at all about him."

"That is like Hans," Ahona said, "he doesn't talk about himself much. He is one of our best lookouts and information gatherers and probably knows more about the Rasset than any other one person."

"He often seems hard and cold," Ahona added, "but it is just defense. He was almost taken by the Rasset who would have tried him and put him to a very slow and painful death because they want to make examples of any they catch who oppose them."

"He always seems so careful. How did they almost catch him?"

"His own son became involved with a Cibth and betrayed him because she made him believe his father was a danger to a peaceful society."

"How could a son do such a thing to his own father? I mean, he must have known what would happen if Hans was caught."

"Oh, he knew all right," Areboh stated. "He claimed he wanted to work with us to return freedom to the Merene. Then one day, with no warning at all, he notified some of the Rasset of his father's location. Hans was taken prisoner and then barely escaped with his life. We needed a place to hide and allow Hans to heal. We did not know about the New Confederates but Accebe's husband, Niltof, knew of them and brought us to one of the Undergrounds. It gave Hans time to heal and we all got involved with the New Confederates."

"Hans has three other sons. It was hard on all of them to have to break totally with the eldest son," Accebe said. "Hans raised his children to be fiercely loyal and come to the aid of any member of the family who needed help. It was a real blow to have family betray family, but the rest of us are even stronger because of it, and heaven help anyone who hurts or endangers any member of the family. We let the traitor live because he was family. Anyone else would not have been as fortunate."

"Don't get the wrong idea," Acir interrupted, "they are a peace seeking family that will go out of their way to help others. But they have a very strong sense of right and wrong and loyalty. I know because I married Hazcra shortly after this all took place."

"So Hanta and Hazcra are also his sons?"

"Yes," Areboh answered, "they are ours as is Haisa. Hans watches our southern edge, Hazcra watches the northern area, Hanta east, and Haisa west. The four of them are our greatest security. They notice things most people would miss, and each of them can handle situations that may arise with a minimum of actions that might alert the Rasset there is anything wrong. This is the first time in a year they have all been here at the same time. None of them has been able to spend much time with his brothers since the Rasset started putting their plans into action."

* * *

Hans, Haisa, Hazcra, and Hanta traveled down the corridor until they reached the central room. The four of them entered through one of three entrances into a large cavern with a raised platform in the center of it. The platform was surrounded by three steps and over it was a large oval that provided light. On the wall opposite the door through which they had entered there was another raised area where six people were seated. Six people who did not look like they had anything in common. A ledge ran around the remainder of the cavern except where the doorways were located. On the ledge thirty-six men were seated.

"Ah, now we can get started," the oldest-looking member of the Council announced. He was a portly man with white hair and beard and what seemed to be a constant smile. "Hans, I understand you have some new information you want to share with us."

"That's right Vadi," Hans said as he strode to the platform and mounted the stairs. "Fellow New Confederates," he began, "due to information I have recently received from an unexpected source, I am afraid we need to speed up our plans. I have reason to believe the rumors we have heard about Mystery Island are true and that the Rasset are planning to establish their headquarters there soon."

"What makes you think that?" asked one of the six on the platform. He had a scruffy, bushy beard that hung almost to his chest and wore a brace on one knee.

"Well Niltof, I found a Vela on the beach in Zone Six."

"You what?" exclaimed the third member loudly as his head came up from looking at some papers he was holding. He was tall with a sour expression on his face and had an unkempt look about him. "How did you manage to find a dead Vela?"

"I didn't say she was dead, Kye."

"She?" the only woman on The Council asked. "Are you referring to the young woman I met earlier in the Meeting Room?"

"Yes, Yamam, and I brought her here so we could get some information and she would be safe. It is a terrific opportunity. We have never been able to talk to anyone who was actually a Vela before."

"What if she's a plant—someone sent to give us false information?" the fifth member of The Council asked. His dark-skinned face showing no emotion.

"Trust me Neliv, she's not."

"What makes you so certain?" the last Council member to speak asked as he ran one hand over his bald head and stroked his sparse beard with the other. He was even taller than Kye.

"Well Dorla, she was in pretty bad shape when I found her, I had a chance to observe her while we traveled here, and I personally removed the disc from her shoulder."

"You mean you were actually able to bring an intact disc here?" Vadi asked as a low murmur from those who were gathered there swept the cavern.

"I brought it here and Haisa has been able to take it apart and figure out how it works. I'll let him fill you in on the details later. Right now I would like your approval to leave the southern edge unguarded while I make a trip to Mystery Island."

"Why is it so important to go right now?" Neliv asked.

"The girl I brought here was being transported in a sky sled. She was to be 'promoted' to the status of Redere. You all know what such a promotion means. The Rasset were transporting four soon-to-be Redere to somewhere and I am almost certain the destination was that island."

"You're right." Niltof said. "If they are moving Redere it means they are close to finishing a headquarters. If that is going to be on Mystery Island it will make any attack against them ten times more difficult."

"We are going to need first-hand information and we are going to need it quickly." Dorla said. "Hans is the one who might be able to get there and back. His uncanny sense of direction is the only way we stand a chance of finding exactly where it is located. When the Rasset began building it, they surrounded the whole area with a fog that never goes away."

"I agree we should send Hans to investigate," Neliv said, "but I would like to send one other in case he runs into trouble. We have no idea what he'll find or what he may encounter."

"I'd rather go alone," Hans stated.

"But what if there's trouble?" Neliv asked. "I don't want anything to happen to one of our best reconnaissance men."

"I appreciate your concern but I will be able to work better if I am alone. If there is someone else I might rely on him at the wrong time and I would always be thinking about his safety as well as my own. Thanks for the offer, but I really need to do this alone."

"Alright," Vadi said, "but we will only be able to allow you five days. That's how long it will take us to step up our plans and get ready to attack the Compounds. We dare not wait any longer than that. If you're not back by then we will have to assume something has happened to you and proceed without you."

"That's a tight schedule but I understand. I'll be back in five days." With that Hans descended the stairs and started toward one of the exits. Part way there he stopped and turned back to face the Council.

"By the way, the girl I brought here has asked to be allowed to stay. Let Hazcra know your decision and he will let her know. She's with Areboh right now."

With that said, he headed for the exit.

"You all know how important the planned attack is," Vadi stated. "If the Rasset establish a headquarters on Mystery Island all our planning and work will have been for nothing. We have to get everything ready in the next five days. Do you all understand?"

Everyone in the chamber nodded their agreement. They all understood only too well what was at stake. If their attack failed, or if the Rasset moved from the Compounds, there would be no second chance.

The plan was to attack all six Compounds at the same time without injuring any Vela. It was believed the Compounds were lightly armed and lightly manned because the Rasset were arrogant. They did not think anyone would dare oppose them.

Two groups from each attacking company were to knock out two diagonally opposite towers quickly and quietly. The remaining two towers would not be able to cover the unprotected area, leaving four sections of the wall that could be scaled easily and the main force would be able to enter without resistance. The whole plan was dependent upon the attack being a total surprise.

"It appears we all need to speed up our plans," Vadi stated. "With the new time schedule, there is no point remaining here any longer. We have planned for this for quite some time now and each of you know what you need to do. The only difficulty is that you have less time to prepare."

"Wait a minute," Yamam spoke up, "what about the girl?"

One of the thirty-six men gathered around the room stood up.

"If Hans will vouch for her, I say we let her stay."

The rest all nodded their agreement.

"Hazcra," Vadi said, "you let her know. Now men, let's get our final preparations under way."

With that the room emptied quickly and quietly.

Hazcra turned to the two standing beside him and stated, "Looks like our mother is going to have a houseguest for awhile."

"You know that will make her happy. She always worries when Hans is gone." Haisa said. "I don't think we should tell her where he's gone though. She wouldn't rest easy at all."

"You're right," Hanta said. "I keep telling her not to worry about him but she just doesn't listen."

"Well, it will be good for both her and Ahe to have someone to keep them occupied while he is gone," Hazcra asserted. "And it will give them an opportunity to teach her about the New Confederates. That will keep them busy. Ahe doesn't admit it, but I think she worries almost as much as mother does. Let's go find out what the women have been up to while we've been gone."

* * *

"What have we missed" Hazcra asked as the three brothers entered Areboh's kitchen and each one grabbed some koieos and sat down.

"We were just talking about our father," Ahe explained.

"He's a good man," Hanta stated.

"And a good father," Hazcra added. Although raising us was not always easy. I remember one time," he began in his best crowd telling voice, "when I lied to him. Oh, it was nothing really big, but he knew I lied. He never said a word to me about it. Then one day I overheard him talking to Haisa and sharing with him about the lie I had told. It was what he said next that really bothered me—he said he was disappointed that I felt I needed to lie to him about anything. That was the day I decided I would never lie to him about anything again. You know, it's kind of funny. I didn't *have* to lie to him because he has a habit of not asking about something that he thinks you might be doing but that could be dangerous or harmful to you. Instead of lying all I needed to do was to say nothing about what I was up to. Oh, I'm pretty certain he would have known—he always seems to know what we boys are doing—or thinking of doing—but my integrity would have remained intact."

"My husband is a very caring man," Areboh added, "not only does he care about his family, he cares a great deal about people. Even though we are Diwesh, Hans does not like violence. He will try every means available to avoid having to resort to physical confrontations. However, there is a point past which he will refuse to try to work out a solution. If, and when, that point is reached, all I can tell you is that it is best to just stand aside."

"That's right," Hanta said, "unlike Hazcra and me, he will not take a life. He refuses to deliver a killing blow. Although it would usually be better for those he goes against if he would because, although he will not kill them, they will usually bleed to death."

"Why does he not kill them then?" Arabella asked.

"None of us—including me—knows the answer to that for certain. Something in his past even before he married me," Areboh answered.

"But wouldn't a quick death be more merciful?"

"Hans always says, 'if there is life, there is a chance of survival'. Enough talking. It's time to feed this poor girl and, unless there has been a sudden change, my boys are all hungry too."

CHAPTER SEVEN

When Hans left the Council Room he headed down one of the eight corridors that radiated out from the central corridor. Moving rapidly, he soon covered the distance to the exit. Touching a stone in the wall, a door opened into a supply room. Having already decided what he would need, he lost no time changing into the gray garb of a fisherman, making certain the hat would keep his hair covered and his eyes in shadow. Then he gathered up the few items he planned to take along with him. He would be safe unless he were stopped and searched and they found the twelve inch long double-edged dagger with an eight inch long blade made of the finest Diwesh steel in the sheath strapped to his thigh under his covering.

Leaving the room he again took the strangely shaped object from his pocket and inserted it into a small opening in the exit door. Rapidly going through the opening, he felt the movement of air as the door shut quickly behind him. His hands found the box of torches just outside the door and, selecting one; he lit a match and touched it to the torch. With the light it provided, he continued down a passageway which was joined by many other passages. Only the New Confederates could travel the maze of tunnels without getting hopelessly lost. Finally, he took a passage that was almost at a right angle to the one he had been traveling and was soon in a small cavern that looked out over the Eastern Sea.

Taking time to survey the area in the light of the setting sun, Hans made certain the dim animal trail he would follow to the stream was empty. Only when he was certain it was safe, did he begin the downward journey. Upon reaching the water's edge he took a dugout from its hiding place and slipped it into the inky water and climbed in. Taking up his paddle he began to propel it into the middle of the stream where the current was strongest. As he headed for the ocean he kept his ears open for any sound that did not belong to the dark night. There was little chance of anyone being on the grass lined riverbanks, but Hans was always cautious. He had to be if he wanted to survive—and he definitely wanted to survive.

Soon reaching the ocean, he headed for the area where Mystery Island was being built. By the middle of the next night he entered the thick fog the Rasset used to keep any chance fisherman from being able to see the island or know anything about it. The fog was so thick that even during midday no one could see through it.

Not able to see anything in the fog and the darkness, he had to rely totally upon his unusual sense of direction. He felt, rather than saw, land ahead. Suddenly the dugout bumped into something and came to a stop. Using the paddle, he maneuvered his craft to be parallel to the shore. Stepping onto solid ground, Hans cautiously made his way along the shoreline. Finding an area of thick brush, he drew the dugout ashore and hid it as best he could in the pitch black darkness. Moving a short distance away, he found a brallem bush. He lay down and rolled under the large, broad leaves that began about waist high to a man and was soon asleep. Long ago he had developed the ability to be able to sleep anywhere and to fall asleep quickly and be able to wake at the slightest unusual noise.

As the first light of day began to illuminate the fog, Hans was up and moving. First, he drank the water collected on one of the large, broad, leaves of the brallem bush. Then he filled his canteen with water from several of the other leaves. Next he made certain the dugout could not be easily seen and there were no signs that anything had been brought ashore. Seeing the dim outline of a hill, he headed straight toward it. There were a series of low hills that were actually piles of imported dirt. Selecting the tallest, Hans headed for the top of it. Fortunately the piles included some large stones so his gray garb blended in well. Moving slowly so as to not draw the attention of anyone who might look in his direction, Hans slowly, carefully made his way to the top.

Most of the terrain had low-growing vegetation but there were occasional clumps of young trees and brallem bushes. Fortunately, all the plant life was fast growing and had already established itself so he was able to move about fairly easily without being seen. He spotted several buildings in the distance at the southern end of the island. Keeping low to the ground, Hans headed for the side of the hill closest to what seemed to be the center of activity. Taking his time, he moved up the hill to gain a better view of the land below. Finding a small recess surrounded by small bushes in the side of the hill, he wedged himself into it and began a careful survey.

They were building an area for sky sleds and pens for the neox. That explained why they had brought over vegetation that would grow quickly and spread rapidly. Neox were easy to handle as long as they were well fed. When they became hungry they were obstinate and sometimes even dangerous. No one wanted to be in the path of a hungry neox.

Hans noted that the areas where trees had been planted were in low spots and out of the way of any sky sleds coming from the mainland. Apparently the plan was to keep a clear line of sight from any part of the island. The Rasset were not taking any chances of an attacker being able to approach undetected even though they were the only ones allowed to have sky sleds.

He spent the whole day carefully learning more about this strange island and looking through his spy glass. The fog actually helped him because it prevented any chance light reflecting off the lens. Although, he did need to be careful because he found that the higher he went the thinner the fog became. Sky sleds would have no problem with visibility. *Smart*, he thought, *the fog prevents everyone else from seeing this island, but the Rasset, with their sky sleds will have no problems at all.*

The island was being built up with dirt brought from the mainland. In fact, the hill he was upon was nothing more than a pile of dirt that had not been moved into place yet. They were using sky sleds to bring the materials in. He was amazed that they had such a large amount of material here already. The New Confederates had only suspected the construction of Mystery Island a short time ago. The Rasset must have been working around the clock for quite some time to bring so much here. He also discovered that this island was actually dirt piled on top of a metal base with sides turned up to keep the dirt from washing away.

Making his way further south, Hans found the main settlement. There were four buildings and they were almost complete. One seemed to be an armory with a narrow bridge from the upper level to the upper level of another building which was probably quarters for the Dura. The third building was only one story high and, judging by the aromas and activity, had to be the kitchen and dining area. The fourth building was three stories high and appeared to have offices or meeting rooms on the lower level and smaller rooms, probably living quarters, on the upper two levels. *How like the Rasset,* he thought, *wanting their living spaces to be above everyone else.*

He noticed a small group of sero, the three-eyed horses used for heavy work. Unlike the small, swift bairan, sero were big. Their shoulders were higher than a man's head and were rarely used for riding because they were so tall and their backs were so broad it made riding uncomfortable. They had probably been brought here to be harnessed to equipment for moving the piles of earth.

By sunset Hans had seen all he could of the southern part of the island. After a final look over the route he intended to take back, he eased himself into a crouching position, moved around to the back of the hill he was on, and began his descent. Traveling to the north, away from the area he had been watching, he continued on until he found another brallem bush close to where he had landed but not the same one he had been under the night before just in case someone had been there and noticed signs of his presence. Moving to the center of the bush, he took another food pouch from his pocket and a small flask of water, ate and then lay down to sleep.

Dawn found him wide awake and refreshed. He refilled his flask with water collected on one of the large leaves of the brallem bush. Taking time to survey the area in all directions to make certain there was no one around, Hans emerged from his hiding and headed north moving from one area of dense vegetation to another, careful not to remain in the open very long in case someone should happen to be looking in his direction. Before long the land leveled off, and the thicker vegetation was almost uninterrupted allowing him to move more quickly.

Hearing a sound ahead he stopped immediately. After only a few moments he saw the form of a niso placidly munching on the foliage. Moving forward he could see a small herd of them in a large open field. *So, they will have an ample food supply,* he thought.

He spent the day scouting the entire northern end of the island. Apparently it was to be used for farming and niso herds. There was not a building of any kind except one shed of farming equipment. Reaching the extreme northern end just before sundown, Hans found a good spot to sleep for the night, ate another quick meal and rolled up in his fisherman's cloak and was soon asleep.

Rising at first light, Hans headed south along the shoreline. By midday he was close to where he had left the dugout. Before heading for it he climbed up one of the low hills so he could survey the area first. Seeing nothing, he began his descent but suddenly felt the presence of someone nearby. Taking care not to reveal he was aware of them, Hans began slowly moving down the steepest side of the hill. After making a couple of switchback turns that any observer would assume were simply a method to keep from gaining too much momentum, he caught a slight movement higher up and following his descent.

He continued down, but altered the direction slightly so he would pass by another brallem bush. When he reached it he was out of sight of his follower for a brief moment. That was all he needed. He ducked under the large leaves, drew his Diwesh dagger from its sheath, lay prone on the ground and waited.

He could see his follower clearly now. It was an Olo. He could tell by the large ears that protruded from the sides of its head at an angle and the square jaw and small mouth. Olo had pale eyes and their heads were covered with fuzz. They were slow thinkers who could be easily swayed by the smooth talking suggestions of a Cibth and, once an Olo accepted an idea, it was almost impossible to change its one-track mind.

This confirmed Hans' suspicions that a Cibth was working with the Rasset. Olo did not involve themselves in the affairs of others unless prompted by a Cibth. This particular Olo was probably working for the Rasset in hopes of being accepted by them and gaining some position of importance. Olo loved to feel important.

Hans put the dagger back into its sheath and waited until the Olo passed close to him. Then he reached out, grabbed its ankle and pulled suddenly. The Olo fell, hitting its head on the ground with a thud. Hans dragged him to the middle of the foliage patch and quickly gagged him and tied his hands and feet securely. While he waited for sunset, Hans took out a piece of tanned hide he had brought with him and began to make a map of Mystery Island while the Olo sat and glared at him. As soon as the sun was almost below the horizon, Hans untied the Olo's legs and prodded him to move until they came to where the dugout was hidden. Slipping it into the water, he made the Olo climb in, got in himself, tied his prisoner's legs to the sides of the dugout so he could not jump out, and began to paddle back to the mainland.

* * *

The sky was just beginning to lighten when they reached the cave Hans had left only four days earlier. Upon landing, Hans once again untied the Olo's legs and, again using his dagger for persuasion, headed him toward the cave. Once inside he lit a torch and took a different passage than the one he had traveled before. As they walked the air became cold and damp with an iciness to it. Hans made the Olo continue on until they came to a small cavern.

"Stop here," he said, "and lay down. I need to fix your 'accommodations' before I leave."

Seeing a spark of hope in the pale eyes of the Olo, he added, "Don't worry, I won't be gone long and you won't be escaping either."

He placed a wide leather band around the Olo's chest, just under his arms which were still bound together behind his back. Then he placed another leather band around his ankles. Next, he walked over to two wheels at the ends of two cylinders around which were wound braided ropes. Hans took one rope in each hand, returned to the Olo, turned him face down on the ground, and attached one rope to each leather band. Then he returned to the wheels and turned them until the ropes were tight. As he continued to turn the wheels, the Olo's body was pulled to the edge of a pit and then out into the emptiness. As he hung there, parallel to the ground but too far from the rim of the pit to touch it, the Olo's eyes grew large and his nostrils flared as the icy cold air flowed up from somewhere deep below and assaulted his senses.

"Well, my friend, you will be safe here until I return. Think carefully about answering all of the questions you will be asked when I come back. It would be a shame to have to be suspended there for a long time."

With that he disappeared into the darkness only to return a short time later with Hanta who was carrying the double-bladed axe he usually had slung on his back. Using a pole with a hook on the end of it, Hans snagged the rope and pulled the Olo to the edge of the pit where Hanta could reach him.

Taking the gag from the mouth of the Olo, Hanta asked, "First of all, do you have a name? It would make it easier than to keep saying 'you there'."

"My name is Reke," the Olo replied proudly, "and you will regret ever taking me captive," he stated as he narrowed his hate filled eyes.

"Now why is that Reke?"

"Because there are other Olo working with the Rasset. They are going to make us an important part of their new territory," he said proudly.

"Spoken like a true Olo," Hans stated, "always wanting to be important."

"We *are* important!" the Olo spat out. His pale eyes narrowing even more as his jaw tightened making the squareness of his face more pronounced.

"It might surprise you to know that one of your own is working with the Rasset," he added.

"Tell us something we do *not* know," Hanta replied trying not to give this Olo the satisfaction of knowing he was surprised, "like the name of the Cibth who recruited you."

"Why should I tell you anything? I hate all who are not Olo."

"Or Rasset," he added quickly. "So I have nothing to say to you," he finished defiantly.

"And I hate Olo," Hanta said as he swung his axe and the keen edge sliced through the rope attached to the band around his chest.

Reke gasped, his pale eyes large with panic. Olo love to feel important, but they are cowards at heart. They are dangerous because, although they will never face an enemy, they have no objection to putting a knife in anyone's back.

"Unless you change your mind and answer our questions, your life expectancy will be very short," Hanta continued. "Now, what is the name of the Cibth?"

"She is the mighty Raica," Reke said proudly. The one who knows what is best. The one who can tell what is in the hearts of others."

Hanta looked at Hans. They had heard about Raica. She was as evil and hateful as her mother who had destroyed an entire settlement years ago.

"Now let me down and I might put in a good word for you," Reke stated. "These bindings are hurting me and the air coming up from this pit is like ice. Besides, all the blood is rushing to my head."

"Not so fast," Hanta replied, "first tell us how soon the Rasset plan on moving to Mystery Island."

Hanta was using the Olo's love of talking to obtain as much information as possible. They delighted in telling others whatever they knew because they thought the more they knew, the more important they would appear to others.

"All is almost ready," the Olo said. "In seven days they will begin moving the Vela there to finish the work."

"Who is doing the work now?" Hanta asked. "Why aren't they using Vela labor already?"

"Because the Resistance Inspectors have been conducting this month's accounting of Vela in each Compound. As soon as they are done the Vela will be moved. Now let me down!" he demanded, regaining some of his courage because he had told them much and they must certainly realize how important he was.

"What about the Rederes?" Hans asked.

"The Rasset were beginning to bring some to the island but something went wrong. I do not know what it was but the sky sled never arrived."

"The Rasset must have some idea about what happened"

"They think one of the neox broke from his harness. Runners found the other one dead and pieces of the sky sled scattered along the southern part of Zone Six. There were no survivors. Let me down right now!" Reke said shouting the last two words.

"As you wish," Hanta replied as he swung his axe and cut the remaining rope as if it were a piece of string.

The Olo fell, screaming, into the icy darkness of the pit.

"I do hate the Olo. They are cowards who hide behind women, puffed up with their own deluded sense of importance." Hanta said as he turned, put the axe in a sling on his back, and walked away.

Hans stood looking into the blackness of the pit until the screaming faded in the distance. Only when he could no longer hear it, did he turn and return to the Underground complex.

CHAPTER EIGHT

"Where is Reke?" Raica shouted as she stamped her foot. "Can't that Olo be depended on for anything?"

Like all Cibth, Raica was short, had a small pointed nose, a mouth that seemed too large for her face, and ears with lobes that hung down to her shoulders. Her dark eyes were cold and expressionless.

"Please do not let it upset you my darling," Hepnet said apologetically, wringing his hands in a subservient manner as he had gotten in the habit of doing shortly after he joined with this Cibth because it seemed to calm her somewhat whenever she was upset—which seemed to be anytime things were not going exactly as she wanted them to go.

"The Rasset sent him to the hills to find a sero that had wandered through an unfinished part of the fence," he continued. "I thought he would be back last night. He must have been too far away to make return before nightfall. You know how the Olo will not travel in the darkness."

"So where is he?" she demanded. "It is almost dark again and I have a task I need him to do for me."

"If he's not back first thing in the morning why don't you have Kar do it for you?"

"I suppose I could. It just infuriates me that I have to use the Olo. They are so unreliable."

"But they are willing to do whatever you ask. Even the menial things that would usually be given to a Vela to do—like chasing a sero. Once the Vela and Redere arrive the Olo will be free to do your bidding. The Rasset will not need them any longer and you will have six Olo to do whatever you wish," Hepnet said hoping the thought would please her and calm her down somewhat.

Raica gave him a cold smile. She always enjoyed being placated by this Diwesh. Unlike the others of his race, he was almost as easily duped as the Olo and it gave her great pleasure to have the son of the man who had defied her mother so totally under her control. She delighted in making him do things because he would instantly do whatever she asked without any question.

She walked out the doorway to look at the last light fading from the misty sky. As she left him standing in their room alone she thought about how the gods had smiled on her—even though she did not believe in any god herself she was quick to use them in her efforts to manipulate others. Who would have ever guessed that a Cibth would be able to lure a Diwesh and so entangle him with her lies and cunning that he would betray and abandon his people to be with her.

The Rasset welcomed Hepnet because of the fighting skill and warfare strategy the Diwesh were noted for. To have a Diwesh planning their defenses and, if need be, leading and fighting with the Dura, had given them a sense of security. Hepnet's presence had made the Rasset more willing to accept Raica. Mistakenly thinking he was the dominant one of the pair, they welcomed him and tolerated her.

A smile crossed the lips of her large mouth as she thought how easily she had gained access to information that was vital to *her* plans. Normally the Rasset would have been cautious about allowing a Cibth to know anything about what they were planning because the Cibth were often trying to create trouble between the other races for their own purposes. They usually succeeded because of their ability to lie and twist the truth without being suspected of doing so. However, by allowing them to think Hepnet, and not her, was in charge, the Rasset quickly dismissed her presence in their meetings. Playing the part of a loving wife, she was able to hear much and adjust her plans accordingly.

The fools, she thought, *if they only knew how their pitiful plans are of no importance other than to help me achieve my purposes. As soon as they establish their headquarters here on Mystery Island I will be free to make my move. Soon.* She told herself. *Soon.*

Returning to their room, she found Hepnet sound asleep. Little did he realize what a pawn he was in her plans. All Cibth were women. Men were used only to provide daughters who were carefully instructed and trained.

She had always despised her own weak father and her husband was no different in her opinion.

Early the next morning, Raica was awakened by a light tapping on the door to their quarters. Hepnet continued his snoring as she got up from the bed and opened the door to find the Olo named Sury standing there.

"You said to tell you when the Rasset were going to meet again."

"When and where?"

"Today at midday"

"Is Hepnet to be there?"

"They will be sending someone to get him soon."

"Good," she said as the cold smile crept across her wide lips, "I will make certain we are both ready. Thank you Sury, the gods will hear of your loyalty."

"From your mouth to their ears," he said as he bowed before turning away and scurrying down the corridor. He truly believed the Cibth had influence upon the various gods the Olo believed in. Convinced by the Cibth that the gods were often angry, the Olo were willing to do whatever a Cibth asked in hopes they would put in a good word for them with the gods.

"Get up you lazy lout," Raica said as she slapped the bare foot protruding from the covers. "We do not want the Rasset to think you are as lazy as you really are."

"What is the rush my darling?" Hepnet asked sleepily.

"A messenger will be here shortly to call you to a meeting today. I want you to be the one to answer the door and I want you to be looking like the handsome, dashing man you are," she purred, knowing she was appealing to his vanity whenever she spoke of his appearance. He was so vain it was easy to manipulate him.

"Now hurry up and get dressed while I get myself ready," she said as she exited the room.

* * *

Only moments after Hepnet was dressed, a Rasset came down the corridor; heels smartly clicking on the stone floor, and came to a stop in front of Hepnet's door. After rapping smartly on the heavy wood, he waited until the door swung open.

"Your presence is required in the main room within the hour," he stated simply.

"Thank you for leaving your other duties to bring a message to an unworthy one like me," Hepnet replied. "You do me a great honor. Assure them we will be there."

With that the door swung shut and the Rasset, pleased with Hepnet's words, walked away wondering why Raica always had to go with her husband when he met with the Rasset. He did not trust her; in fact, he did not even like her.

As they entered the room, Raica was holding her husband's arm and looking very small and uninterested in anyone except him. The Rasset did not give her a second thought. They had grown accustomed to her constant presence because Hepnet seemed to go nowhere without her.

The Leader, a tall, white-haired individual who looked imposing in his purple robe, stood at the head of a large wood table around which were gathered six Retona, the most important Rasset of each Zone, each wearing a purple robe and gold medallion. All, save one, with white hair. The overall impression was one of wisdom, dignity, and power—exactly the image they always worked hard to create.

"Hepnet, we're glad you could join us on such short notice. We have concluded that the accident involving the sky sled and four Redere was the result of too much cargo for a tired neox to handle. Therefore, we have decided to use more sky sleds for the mass transport. This may alert the Resistance to the fact that something is going on, so we will need you to lead a distraction that will keep them from noticing."

"Did you have anything particular in mind?" Hepnet asked.

"Yes. If you could find one of those rebels and accuse him of plotting against us and breaking the Treaty, the Resistance would have no choice but to investigate, and that would keep their focus off the Compounds while we move the Vela and Redere to this island."

"That might not be easy. The rebels are pretty careful."

"That is why we are looking to you. With your knowledge of them and their ways, and your Diwesh training, you are probably the one most able to bring it about."

"How soon are you planning on moving the Vela?"

"Right after the next inspection, which is in seven days."

"I'll head for the mainland first thing in the morning."

"Good," the Leader said with a broad smile which did not quite reach his cold, dark eyes. "Now let's all head for the dining room. I have requested a special menu to celebrate the near completion of Mystery Island and the soon arrival of the Redere which will insure a steady supply of delicacies."

Raica cringed ever so slightly. The menu of the Rasset turned her stomach, but they considered it an honor to be invited to one of their meals and she dared not offend them—yet.

* * *

When they returned to their room after the dinner, Raica turned on her husband and said, "What were you thinking? How do you plan to draw out one of the rebels? Do you not remember what happened the last time you had any contact with them?"

"I remember very well," he replied meekly, "but I thought you might be able to think of some way. Perhaps we could use one of the Olo to appeal to them for help. You know what suckers they are for people who need help."

"I do not plan on going with you," she said arrogantly. "I have absolutely no desire to risk any possible contact with any of your people unless they are prisoners. Besides, there are important things I must be doing here."

"We tried making them prisoners once and it failed," Hepnet replied.

"Don't *ever* say that again!" she screamed at him. "The failure was not mine. It was the imbeciles who were to bring them in who failed. That stupid Retona, Sona, bungled everything."

"Yes my darling. I did not mean to upset you. It was an excellent plan and should have worked perfectly. Hans should have been killed. Sona failed you."

"That's right," she retorted. "We could have crushed the Resistance and the Rasset would have been next." The last five words were spoken softly, almost in a whisper.

"You will have to go without me," she continued. "I will stay here to make certain nothing interferes with my plans. Just be careful not to get into a situation you cannot get yourself out of. These Rasset think you are actually competent. They do not realize how helpless you are without me."

Hepnet's jaw tightened but he said nothing. He always thought of himself as quite clever and had learned the fine art of lying convincingly long ago. He had also learned not to argue with his volatile wife.

"I shall try my best my darling," was all he said as he began assembling the few things he intended to take with him.

"I will take Kar with me. I may need his help and he follows orders very well."

"He is stupid, but useful. Take him but do not trust him too much and wear the amulet. It will remind him you are a representative of the gods."

"I will. Do not worry my darling. I shall return in a few days."

"Just be careful. We still do not know where Hans is, or what he is up to. As long as he is free to move about as he wishes I cannot rest easy."

"He would never hurt me," Hepnet stated.

"Do not underestimate him," Raica continued, "that was my mother's mistake. He is nowhere near as simple as you would like to believe him to be."

* * *

No sooner had Hepnet and Kar departed in one of the sky sleds the next morning than the Olo named Rahete was knocking on Raica's door. Upon opening the door, Raica could see she was upset. Tears were welling up in the Olo's pale eyes and, noticing the quivering of her square jaw, Raica took her by the hand and drew her inside.

"Come in and tell me what's wrong," she invited.

"You must ask the gods to tell you what has happened to Reke. I fear it is something terrible and do not understand why they would cause anything to happen to him. He has done nothing wrong."

"Why do you think something has happened to him?"

"Three days ago he was sent to find a sero that had wandered to the northern end of the island and he has not returned. That is not like him. I just know something bad has befallen him."

Rahete was in tears and Raica knew she must calm her somehow. "Perhaps he has simply suffered some minor injury that has slowed him down. I will ask the gods when I commune with them this afternoon. I dare not disturb them now lest they become angry and truly do harm Reke."

Raica was certain something had indeed happened to him but she was stalling. She needed some time to investigate and decide how to place any blame on something someone had done to upset the gods.

"Return to your quarters and offer prayers to all of the gods—make certain you neglect none of them—and I will let you know what I hear later today."

Rahete seemed reassured. Thinking this powerful Cibth would intercede on her behalf; she ceased her crying and obediently headed back to her own quarters.

As soon as Rahete left, Raica quickly dressed in riding attire and headed for the Rasset's main rooms. Encountering the Leader on his way out of the building, she meekly asked if she might be allowed to take one of the sero and look for Reke.

"Why bother yourself with on Olo? They are so stupid he probably fell into a hole and cannot get out," the Leader said, his disregard for the Olo obvious.

"It would calm the other Olo" she said, "and with Hepnet gone I have little else to do."

"Do you know how to ride a sero and keep it under control?"

"Yes, Leader, I have been taught by one of the best," she responded, keeping her anger hidden. What made this man think he had the right to question her?

"Very well, but make certain you return before dark. If you do not, these superstitious Olo will be convinced some great disaster is about to befall us."

"Thank you, Leader," she purred.

"While you are about it, look for the sero he was sent to find."

"Yes, Leader, as you wish," she said meekly even though she was fuming to think that he would ask *her* to do a task he had given to an Olo!

She quickly went to the pasture and sweetly asked one of the Rasset to place a riding platform upon the wide back of a sero. When he complied, she smiled pleasantly at him and climbed up on the platform. Kneeling on the cushion in the center of the wide riding platform, she took the wide reins in her hands, tapped the rear of the sero to let it know she wanted it to go forward, and was soon out of the settlement area and headed north.

The Rasset could not help smiling as he watched such a tiny figure ride away on such a large beast.

* * *

"Gentlemen—and lady," Hans said as he addressed the Council and the thirty-six Zone representatives with Hazcra, Hanta, and Haisa standing beside him, "our fears were not unfounded. Mystery Island is large and it is almost complete. They also have some Olo and a Cibth working with them."

"A Cibth?" Yamam asked. "I thought they had left this area several years ago."

"I am afraid this one may be here because of me."

"You?" Dorla asked. "What would a Cibth want with you?"

"Revenge. Many years ago I revealed her mother's motives and evil intentions and a Cibth neither forgets nor forgives."

"Well, if a Cibth is involved we will all need to be even more cautious," Neliv said. "Their hate and ambition know no limits."

"I do not know any Cibth," Kye stated, "aren't you all overreacting?"

"No," Vadi replied, "they are pure evil. Hans, Yamam, and I can all attest to that."

"As can I," Niltof added. "Although I have had no direct contact with them, I know some who have and it is always the same—unimaginable viciousness and cruelty."

"Well," Hans continued, "as long as she remains on the island we should not have too much to worry about. I simply wanted all of you to know the possible danger. Now, how are the preparations coming?"

"All six of our militia groups are ready," Vadi replied. "The four of you will each lead one. Niltof and Neliv will lead the other two."

"It is important that all six attacks take place at the same time," Niltof added, "or the Rasset will have opportunity to regroup and get the Resistance involved because we will be violating the terms of the Treaty."

"We want to remove the threat of the Rasset without alienating the Resistance. We would like them to help form the New Confederacy," Yamam stated. "There are some very good men among the Resistance."

Hazcra spoke up and said, "I have developed a crossbow which will shoot six arrows, one after the other, without reloading."

"And," Haisa continued, "I have made six devices which should interfere with the signal the Rasset use to activate the discs. I wish I could have tested them first, but I am certain they will interfere with, if not totally block, the signal."

"Enough talking," Hanta interrupted, "let us hurry to our places and finish preparations. We must strike in three days and my axe is thirsty for Rasset blood."

"As is my scimitar," Haisa added.

"And I have some new explosives I am anxious to use. I have given some to each group and will enjoy seeing the night sky lit by their detonation," Hazcra stated.

"It seems our Diwesh allies are tired of waiting," Dorlah stated, "and I must confess that I am as well. Let us delay no longer."

"All in agreement," Vadi said, "rise and take up your weapons."

They all stood.

"May Nido watch over all of us and give us victory and protection," Hans said solemnly.

Unlike the Olo, the Diwesh believed in only one god and, unlike the gods of the Olo, Nido did not interfere in men's lives nor did he use them to amuse himself. The god of the Diwesh asked for honesty, sincerity, and valor; and honored those who displayed such traits.

CHAPTER NINE

Cibth were not very good at tracking someone. They relied more upon their ability to manipulate others than on being able to follow where someone had gone. However, following where an Olo had travelled was not a difficult task. Shortly after leaving the settlement area, Raica found the path Reke had taken three days earlier. Riding upon the sero, she was able to travel swiftly, although not comfortably, and by midday had found where he had caught the missing sero. Reke had tied part of its mane in one end of a rope and then tied the other end around a small tree. Although the sero could have easily pulled the tree out by the roots, sero did not like anything that pulled at their mane so, even after three days, it remained tied.

Why didn't you just head back? Raica wondered. Lowering a rope ladder from the wide riding platform, she dismounted and began looking around to see if she could discover where Reke had gone after tying the sero. She could see signs indicating he had continued north, but why? What would have caused him to keep going when he should have simply returned to the settlement? Olo were not very brave, even though they liked to consider themselves so, but they were very curious. If he had seen something unusual, his curiosity would have prompted him to continue on, but what could he have seen on this island that would distract him from doing what he was sent to do?

After thoroughly looking, and finding nothing, she returned, untied the sero, kept one end of the rope in her hand, remounted her own animal, and headed back to the settlement.

As she rode, her mind was busy planning what she would tell Rahete and how she could blame Reke's disappearance on someone upsetting the gods. Rahete always tried to appease the gods and was certain she never did anything to incur their disfavor. So Raica dared not try to accuse her of offending them. Perhaps she could lay the blame on Elacha, the Olo the others thought of as a rebel. Although Elacha went through the motions of honoring the gods, she never showed proper respect for them. In fact, she was more concerned with receiving the attention of others herself than with keeping the favor of the gods. Yes, that was it. She would tell Rahete and Sasice that their sister, Elacha, had, once again, done something to upset the gods and now they were punishing the other five Olo who tolerated her disregard for them. It would also help Raica gain more control over the unpredictable Elacha.

* * *

Upon returning to the settlement, Raica went straight to her quarters, washed up and changed into the white robe she preferred to wear whenever she was appearing as a priestess of the gods and placed the large, round, gold amulet around her neck, making certain it could be easily seen by all, and pulled the hood over her head.

When she arrived at the rooms the Olo shared, she knocked softly on the door and waited. When it opened she stepped inside and said nothing until Rahete, Sasice and Elacha were all gathered together.

"Well, I have communed with the gods on your behalf," she began in a calm voice, "and they have revealed to me the reason they are angry with you and this is further proof their anger is not unfounded."

Turning to face Elacha, her voice rose and her tone hardened as she continued. "You have repeatedly failed to honor the gods. You are more concerned with yourself than with giving them honor. They know you do not fear them and even dare to defy them!"

Suddenly realizing one of the Olo was missing, she demanded, "Where is Sury?"

"He has left on a sky sled for the mainland," Rahete replied.

"Who told him to go to the mainland?" Raica asked, trying very hard to keep her voice calm and not reveal her anger at learning that an Olo had gone anywhere without her knowledge.

"He asked the Leader for permission to go with the work sleds when they left for one more load of dirt to build the island."

Raica was suddenly very wary. Olo did not volunteer for anything which might involve work.

"Why did he ask to go?"

"He and Elacha had a terrible fight last night," Sasice said.

"When is he to return?"

"We have no idea. The last time they fought he stayed away for days," Sasice replied with a sadness in her voice.

Ah, this is working out better than I hoped, Raica thought.

"So you have no idea when your mate will come back to you?"

"No," Elacha replied sullenly, "I was angry with him and he left right after the midday meal without saying a word."

"Well, I shall have to learn what I can from the Rasset and the gods themselves. But do not be surprised if they have taken him from you because of your stubbornness and vanity," Raica said hoping the recent events, and her words, would result in this troublesome Olo being easier to control.

Turning to face the other two, Raica went on to say, "I am afraid the gods will cause more harm to befall you before their anger is appeased."

"But you must be able to do *something* to calm their anger," Rahete said as Elacha stood there, her defiance showing in her pale eyes and the clenched teeth which only emphasized the squareness of her jaw.

"I am afraid there is nothing I can do. When the gods become angry they listen to no one until their anger abates."

"Did you learn anything about Reke?" Rahete asked hopefully.

"They would not speak to me about him. I am afraid you were right and something terrible has befallen him." She knew that his long absence and failure to return to where he had tied the sero could only mean something had indeed happened to him.

"Is there nothing we can do then?" Sasice asked. "I am afraid for Kar while he is away."

"While the gods are angry there is nothing any of us can do. Even offerings such as the one I gave today will go unnoticed. Our fates are in their hands. All we can do is to make certain we do not upset them further."

* * *

"I am going with you," Ahe stated definitely as soon as Hans entered his living quarters after the meeting with the Council. "You need all the archers you can get and you know I can shoot as well as any of the men.

Besides," she added, "I helped Hazcra develop the new crossbows and have been shooting them longer than anyone else."

Areboh looked from her daughter to her husband. She knew Ahe was right and she knew her husband's desire to keep his youngest from danger. She could tell he was struggling with her request.

Ahe would honor her father's decision, but she desperately wanted to be a part of defeating the Rasset.

"Her sister, Accebe, will be fighting alongside Niltof, Ahona will be with Hanta, and Acir will be with Hazcra," Areboh stated. "As much as I want her to stay here with me, she would be a help to you and she *is* Diwesh."

"Your brothers will not be there to protect you," Hans said as he looked at his daughter through serious eyes. "There will be much danger."

"I know, but we must each take our part in this battle. My brothers have all taught me much, and that knowledge will enable me to do whatever needs to be done."

He knew she was right, but he dreaded the thought of his youngest daughter going into battle. It was not the same as hunting for food. After her first battle she would never be the same. To kill an animal for food is one thing; to kill a man in order to survive is quite another.

"Get your bow and arrows," Hans said with a resigned sigh. "We must be going."

Arabella watched as Hans took his wife in his arms and they just held one another. No words were necessary. They stood together for long moments, seeming to draw strength from each other.

Finally Areboh softly said, "I wish you did not have to go."

"But you know I must," he replied as he went to the corner of the room and picked up his sword and scabbard and slung it on his back. Then draped a cloak over his shoulder to conceal the sword.

"I know," she said sadly. "Return to me quickly and unharmed."

"You know I shall do my best," he said showing his slight grin as he turned and headed for the door with Ahe.

"How can you let him go," Arabella asked as the door closed behind them, "knowing the danger he might face."

"I have loved him for many years. He is a man with a strong sense of right and wrong, and if he did not do all he could to oppose the wrong, he would stop being himself. I could never ask him to be less than what he is."

"How do you endure the uncertainty, the not knowing if he will return?"

"I spend much time talking to Nido. He watches over all my men. I wish with all my heart they did not have to go to battle and endanger themselves, but they fight for a good cause. I know my husband and my sons and daughters and there is within each of them something that will not allow an evil to go unopposed."

"You are an amazing woman," Arabella said, "I believe I can learn much from you."

"And I welcome the company," Areboh replied.

* * *

Six men and four women made their way cautiously toward their respective Zones. Hanta and Ahona headed north to the Red Zone. Neliv remained in the Blue Zone but carefully made his way to the area near the Compound. Hans and Ahe headed south for the Brown Zone.

The others headed for the Middle Sea and waited for night before crossing. Little did they realize when they landed on the west shore of the Middle Sea in the Black Zone as the sun was beginning to rise that Hepnet and Kar were landing their sky sled at the Compound in that very Zone.

Immediately after hiding their dugout, the five occupants separated. Hazcra and Acir headed north to the Yellow Zone, Niltof and Accebe went west to the Compound in the Black Zone, and Haisa headed south to the Green Zone with his scuzzets in a bag he carried over his shoulder. The scuzzets liked to travel and he liked the companionship. Each party moved quickly but cautiously. They knew the danger of being caught before the attack as well as the danger of the battle to come.

When Haisa approached the Separation between the Black and Green Zones he, like Hans had taught him, took time to carefully survey the entire area. Only when he was certain no one was around did he begin a careful crossing of the barren area. Just as he was about to enter the foliage of the Green Zone, Hepnet and Kar happened to approach the Separation from the north. Simply by chance, Hepnet caught the movement as Haisa was swallowed up by the brush.

"We'll wait until he will not be able to see us cross, and then we'll follow his trail," Hepnet whispered.

Only because he was Diwesh himself was Hepnet able to discern which way Haisa had gone. Following the same faint game trail, Hepnet and Kar proceeded quickly. Hoping the Olo would not make any noise or do anything foolish, Hepnet led the way. He spotted Haisa bending over a small stream filling his canteen; his back was to them. However, Hepnet did not notice the scuzzets drinking from the same stream. Hepnet stopped so suddenly the Olo bumped into him almost knocking him over.

"Don't move Reth," Hepnet proclaimed in his most commanding voice as he and Kar stepped from the brush.

Haisa froze, then rose slowly and turned, cursing himself for allowing anyone to get the drop on him. Had Hans not told him repeatedly to make certain he could see his back trail as well as the trail ahead? Who was this stranger holding a lightweight sword, with an Olo holding a spear standing at his side?

As Haisa stood up Hepnet could see the sheathed scimitar hanging from his waistband.

"How do you come to possess a weapon?" Hepnet demanded.

"I am a Diwesh traveling through your land."

"You are Diwesh?" Hepnet asked, hardly able to suppress his delight at his good fortune. Certainly the gods must be smiling upon him he thought as his fingers subconsciously stroked the gold amulet hanging upon his chest. "You have permission to cross the Separation?"

"I did not realize I needed any permission."

"You will need to come to the Compound with us then."

"I cannot. I have business I need to attend to."

"That is most unfortunate. It will have to wait until the Rasset have given you permission."

Hepnet could hardly contain himself. He pictured himself walking into the Compound with a Diwesh prisoner and accusing him of plotting to break the Treaty. The Leader would be so pleased and Raica would see just how clever he was and how the gods were blessing him.

"Hand over your weapon and let us get on our way," he said to Haisa as Kar started to move toward him pointing his spear menacingly.

"Stay where you are Olo," Haisa snapped. "You have not identified yourself," he said to Hepnet. "Nor have you said which Zone you are authorized to act in. Perhaps it is *I* who should be taking *you* to the Rasset."

Hepnet was astounded. How did this man dare question him!

"I am operating under the direction of the Leader himself," he stated proudly.

"You? You are not Rasset. Why would the Leader use you, and what authority did he give you that includes more than one Zone?"

"That is none of your affair," Hepnet snapped, angry at meeting resistance to his plans.

"Then my business is none of your affair either," Haisa replied. "Move aside and I will be on my way."

Hepnet was furious. He was not accustomed to facing opposition and hated anyone who dared question his importance.

"Kar, take his weapon," he snapped.

As the Olo began to move toward him again, Haisa drew the scimitar so quickly that before the Olo even realized what had happened, blood was flowing from a deep gash across his belly. Dropping his spear, Kar futilely tried to stop the bleeding and hold his intestines in with both hands.

"Now," Haisa said as he faced Hepnet, the tip of his scimitar pointed threateningly toward him, "sheathe your sword, stand aside, and allow me to pass. Or do you also desire to taste the metal of my scimitar?"

Hating himself for not having the courage to face this man alone, Hepnet clenched his teeth in anger and obeyed the command. He had never fought alone and dared not do so now.

As he looked at his opponent, Haisa noticed his eyes were two different colors.

"You are Diwesh!" he exclaimed. "What are you doing helping the Rasset?"

"I have renounced the Diwesh," Hepnet spat. "You are all dreamers and fools. I am much wiser than any of you and long after you are gone they will sing the praises of the great Hepnet, the one who aided the Rasset."

"You are Hepnet?" Haisa asked softly.

"Ah, you have heard of me already then?"

"Yes, I have heard of the coward and traitor named Hepnet," he said as he made a quick motion with his left hand. Immediately the scuzzets leapt upon Hepnet's legs and scurried up his body in a circular route until they came to his shoulders. As they bit into his flesh with their sharp teeth he screamed in pain but they would not let go.

"Drop your sword and I will call them off," Haisa said calmly.

"So you can kill me?" he asked through clenched teeth.

"I will not kill Diwesh—even a traitorous one—unless it is on the battlefield. Now hurry and drop your sword or the teeth of the scuzzets will draw even more blood."

Letting the sword fall to the ground, Hepnet glared as his foe picked it up and threw it back down the trail in the direction from which he had come.

Haisa gave a low whistle and the two scuzzets scampered back down and climbed into the bag which he picked up and slung over his shoulder.

"Do what you can to make your Olo comfortable. Not even they should die alone in agony."

"We will meet again," Hepnet growled holding his hands to his shoulders.

"I look forward to it," Haisa replied as he headed into the brush and quickly sped away.

"Help me," Kar called out in anguish.

"I can do nothing for you," Hepnet snarled as his anger grew even greater in intensity. "You failed me. I shall make certain to tell Raica to ask the gods to curse you for your incompetence as you enter the hereafter.

CHAPTER TEN

The next day Sasice and Rahete came to Raica's room bringing a reluctant Elacha with them. Sasice was in tears.

"What is it? What has happened?" Raica asked.

"I do not know," Sasice replied. "I only know that something terrible has happened to Kar."

"How do you know this?" Raica demanded.

"I just feel it. I was working this afternoon and suddenly I felt a tremendous loss—an emptiness that I have never felt before."

"I told her I felt the same way the night after Reke did not return" Rahete added.

"Do not be foolish. Kar is with Hepnet and they will be returning soon. However, there is no telling what the gods will allow to happen if Elacha continues her disregard of them and of my instructions. I shall have to petition the gods on your behalf once more and I will also try to learn from the Rasset when Sury will be returning. Go back to your jobs and do them unusually well. We cannot afford to anger the Rasset as well. Now go. I have much to do today."

The three Olo quickly exited the room and Raica began preparing herself. Although most of the Rasset simply tolerated her presence, there was one who seemed to enjoy her being around. She had been aware of his glances on several occasions. Now she planned to use his interest to her advantage. She opened the box in which were vials of different fragrances she wore depending upon her mood and the occasion. She selected the one the Rasset called Eono had once mentioned he liked, and applied it. By the time she exited her room in her white robe, complete with amulet and hood, she had a definite plan in mind.

Heading straight to the large room set aside for the Rasset to relax and amuse themselves with various games and activities, Raica quickly scanned the faces of those there. If she truly believed in any gods she would have prayed to them before arriving. Not seeing Eono in the room, she was about to leave when she noticed a solitary figure enter through a side doorway. It was Eono and he was alone. Quickly making her way across the room to him, she smiled her most pleasant smile.

"Eono," she purred in her softest voice, "I was hoping to find you here. I must speak to you—alone."

The Rasset looked down at her uplifted face and hesitated only a moment before replying.

"We can go to my quarters and talk freely."

"Thank you my lord."

He turned and began to lead the way with Raica following meekly behind as befitted anyone traveling with a Rasset. They climbed a flight of stairs, traveled down a well-lit corridor, and stopped in front of the door to Eono's quarters. He stood beside it and motioned for her to enter, then closed the door behind him and gestured toward a plush chair close to the one he headed toward.

Raica remained standing. To sit in the chair he had indicated would have required a footstool or someone to assist her because her legs were too short to allow her to sit down gracefully in seats made for those of average height. Hepnet was usually along to lift her onto a seat. A quick look around the room made Raica jealous. He was the only resident of these quarters and yet they were twice as large as the ones she and Hepnet had been given. Quickly hiding her anger, she turned to face Eono. He was, like most Rasset, of average height—which made him almost twice as tall as her—with dark hair and eyes, and a face which seemed to never be visited by a smile. He was not unhandsome, she decided and, under different circumstances, she might even have considered a relationship with him.

"What is it you wish to speak to me about?" he asked in the calm voice Rasset always tried to use. They considered it a weakness to show any emotion or excitement to those who were not Rasset.

"My lord, as you know, I have been given the responsibility of watching over the Olo. They do not work overly hard under the best of circumstances and, right now, they are becoming distressed. I fear that if I cannot calm them, they will be so fretful they will be of little use to you. I understand the Leader gave one of them permission to go to the mainland with one of the work sleds. His mate is afraid he does not intend to return."

"The Leader informed us of this at our morning meeting," Eono said. "Although I appreciate the difficulty you are in, I can do nothing to change the situation. The Olo of whom you refer asked to be allowed to return to his homeland and the Leader thought it better to grant the request than have one here who would be causing trouble. I am afraid you must do what you can to calm the rest of them."

"Yes my lord," she replied, very aware of the attention his eyes were giving her and thinking how helpful it might prove to be to her plans to have one of the Rasset as an ally.

"Unfortunately," he continued, "there are matters to which I must attend today. However, I would like to learn more about you. You are a Cibth and I know so little about them. Perhaps we can meet again when we both have more time."

Not many males were attracted to Cibth, but Raica knew when one was, and she knew the best ways to manipulate and use them.

"That would be delightful," she purred, lowering her eyelids in false modesty. "I would enjoy being with you again soon."

Eono rose from his seat in such a way as to pass close to her.

"You must also tell me what fragrance you wear. It is a delightful odor; one that lingers long after you have gone. I am confident that when I return to my quarters later the aroma will remind me of our short time together."

Raica smiled. *This man can easily be made into a pawn,* she thought.

* * *

That evening Raica, still attired in her white robe, amulet, and hood, went to the Olo's quarters.

"The gods will tell me nothing about Kar," Raica announced. "However, I did learn that not only has Sury gone to the mainland, he also requested to be allowed to return to his own country."

"Why?" Elacha asked, her voice choking with emotion.

"He stated he would rather dwell in his cold northern country than stay with you any longer," Raica replied, pointing a finger at her.

"But I love him."

"No, you love you," was the harsh rebuttal, "a fact known by the gods themselves as well as any who have known you for any length of time."

"Can't you petition the gods to bring him back?" Sasice asked.

"Yes. But I will not because they would consider such a petition a waste of their time. Why should they interfere in the affairs of a stubborn, selfish, hard to get along with, vain Olo?"

"You are not being very nice," Rahete stated.

"I am being honest," Raica snapped.

"Now we must discuss more important issues," she continued in a more soothing voice.

"Reke is missing, Sury is gone, and Kar is with Hepnet. We are free to plan without the interference of any of them."

"What do you mean 'plan'?" Rahete asked.

"Do you really think a Cibth is going to allow the Rasset to tell her what to do? We must make our move soon before they have time to realize that it will soon be me, and not them, directing the affairs of the Merene. The first thing we must do is destroy the New Confederates and I have already sent Hepnet to start that. He thinks he is serving the Rasset and feels very important, but he is simply a pawn in my game. Now, the three of you can help me further the demise of any resistance. I need each of you to approach one of the Rasset and tell them you have just received information that the New Confederates are a threat to them. Tell them a Diwesh named Hans is their leader and must be destroyed. All of the Retona are here right now and if you can get their ear they will move to action quickly."

The Retona were the heads of the Zones. In addition to the purple robe worn by all Rasset, the Retona wore a gold medallion around their neck so everyone would know how important they were. They never went anywhere without a Rasset to attend to their needs and a Dura to protect them from any danger. Dura were allowed to wear the purple robes of the Rasset, but had to have their heads shaved at all times lest anyone think they were Rasset. Only Dura were allowed to carry weapons.

"Why do we need to do this?" Rahete asked.

"Because the gods have commanded us to do this on their behalf."

"Why don't the gods do it themselves?" Elacha asked sullenly.

"Don't be a fool," Raica snapped, hating this troublesome Olo. "The gods do not interfere in matters we can take care of ourselves. We are to serve them, not ask them to serve us."

"When are we to begin?" Sasice asked.

"First thing in the morning. Rahete, you can even add that you fear they might have harmed Reke. That might move them to action all the faster."

* * *

The night before the planned attack, there were six small groups in locations around each of the Compounds. The leader of each group made their way to a rendezvous location to meet with the commander for their Zone. Tonight they did not wear the coverings imposed by the Rasset. Instead each wore the traditional attire of the Merene, thick leggings and leather vests over tunics.

Ahe sat by the fire with her father as he and the leaders of the attack on the Brown Zone Compound once more reviewed their plans.

"You all know how important it is that this attack succeeds," Hans stated. "You must also remember that some of our men will die tomorrow night. It is a terrible thing to lose a friend or a family member, but we must keep our focus on the objective. If a brother, son, father, or friend should fall in battle; you must not stop to try to help them. That must wait until the battle is over. Even if those on each side of you fall, you must continue on."

"We know this," one of the men replied quietly, "and we are ready for tomorrow night."

"Physically and mentally you are ready," Hans stated. "Emotionally you can never be ready. It is indeed a terrible thing to see a man die. It is even more terrible to see a man, or a woman, enslaved by those who would misuse their power to oppress others."

They all nodded their agreement.

"That is why we enter this battle," he continued. "No man, or group of men, has the right to make others his slaves. Nido did not create us to live in bondage and he is not pleased when it happens. We will be fighting against men who have become so perverted in their way of thinking that they do not even value another's life. You may have heard that we Diwesh are fierce fighters. Although that is true, we value each life and regret situations such as we now face where we must either yield to those who would make slaves of everyone, or risk our own lives as we seek to take theirs."

Ahe watched the faces of the men gathered around the small fire and saw the somber expressions as they were reminded of what each of them knew, but tried to keep buried in their subconscious. There was no guarantee any of them would be sitting by a fire after the attack. There was no assurance any of them would not lose a friend or loved one. She realized, more than ever before, why Hans always tried so hard to reach peaceful solutions.

She looked at the sword strapped to his back and, although she knew it had been used in many battles, she had never realized what it cost him emotionally each time he used it. It was three feet long and fullered for lightness. Although many called the fuller a "blood groove", that was not the reason for it. The groove decreased the weight of the blade without diminishing its strength or structural integrity. The wood scabbard the sword was kept in was lined with wool so the natural greases protected the metal of the blade.

"Each of you has one of Haisa's signal disrupters. Make certain it is turned on as soon as the first explosion goes off. We dare not take the chance that the Rasset will not send out the signal to activate the disks at the first sign of trouble.

"Go to your men now. Encourage each of them. Make certain they get rest. We all need to be ready for tomorrow night. Spend the day preparing for battle. Check and double check all equipment. We must be totally prepared by the time the moon sets."

Hans had learned that, unlike his native country, here the moon rose each night shortly after sunset and after a few hours it also set leaving the remainder of the night very dark and black. It was this quirk of nature that would make their plan possible. Under cover of the dark they would surround the Compound. Two men would then approach each of two opposite towers and plant some of the explosives Hazcra had developed that could be set off from a safe distance. As soon as the explosions had removed the towers, the majority of the men would rush through the openings. Some would remain outside to assist the Vela who would be freed and destroy any who pursued. No Rasset were to be allowed to escape alive.

* * *

In each of the Zones this same type of talk was given to remind each participant of what would transpire the following night.

Niltof could not lead the men into battle because his knee had been damaged in a skirmish when the Rasset first came to power, but he made certain the leaders of each of his six groups understood what needed to be done and how best to accomplish it.

Neliv was old and too slow to lead men into battle, but he too had chosen leaders carefully.

Once the battle began, both of these men would be in a location where they could watch for any who tried to escape. Both had practiced with the new crossbows a great deal, and both were determined to do everything in their power to make certain no Rasset escaped.

* * *

As soon as the moon disappeared below the horizon, sixty men in each Zone moved closer to the Compound in that Zone. One group faced each of the corner towers, one faced the east entrance and one faced the west entrance. The four Diwesh leaders wore their battle attire of a heavy leather breastplate as well as forearm and leg protectors. These were made up of two layers of leather with a thin layer of metal between them. Each carried his weapon of choice and also had a Diwesh dagger strapped to his thigh.

Two men from each group facing the targeted opposing towers continued moving when the rest stopped. They began to silently make their way toward their targets. Each carried a pack with enough explosive to take the tower down and, in case they were spotted, each went by a different route. Each one also carried in his mouth a detonator which could be swallowed if they should be caught. Just one explosive would topple the tower. The second would insure that a hole would be made in the wall.

Upon reaching the enclosure, the explosive was placed exactly where Hazcra had instructed. The detonators were taken from their mouths and placed in the center of the explosive pack. Then they carefully made their way back to their group. It was difficult to resist the urge to run back but they all knew the danger of rushing. To rush would increase the possibility of being seen.

As the quiet of the night was suddenly shattered by explosions, two men from the groups positioned near the remaining two towers quickly made their way to the wall and placed their explosives to take down those towers as well. They did not move as slowly as the first ones had because they knew all the attention in the Compound would be upon the locations of the first explosions.

When the second set of explosions went off, the four groups facing the towers ran for the openings that had been created, hoping the confusion inside the compounds would give them time to enter before being spotted by the Rasset—especially any Dura. Two from each group remained behind, armed with the new crossbows, and watched for any Rasset who fled or attempted a rear attack. Accebe, Acir, Ahona, Ahe, Niltof, and Neliv were some of these watchers. The other two groups quickly spread out along the east and west side to watch for any purple robed figures who might try to escape.

* * *

Leading the charge in his Zone, Hans took the broadsword from its sheath as soon as he climbed over the rubble. With a valiant man on each side, he began cutting a path of destruction. As quickly as they could, each man who came through one of the four openings in the wall took a position alongside his comrades and the four lines thus formed moved steadily toward the center of the Compound where the Vela were kept. One archer in each group stayed just inside each opening to remove any threat from a Rasset along the walls, thus insuring no attack from the rear was possible.

As he moved forward, Hans felt the rage that he had kept bottled up inside himself for so long loosed within him. The first Dura he encountered had no time to react as Hans swung his broadsword with the fierce passion born of a hatred for any who would oppress others. Before the Dura knew what was happening, his arm was severed from his body. Hans' face was emotionless as he looked at his fallen foe and continued on toward his objective. Each time the broadsword was swung, it removed an arm, a leg, or a hand and left a man clutching his dismembered limb, screaming in agony and trying to stop the flow of blood. Spattered with blood, Hans continued to move toward the Vela housing showing no mercy for any who stood in his way.

All four lines moved forward relentlessly until they arrived at their destination. Quickly opening the doors, the New Confederates rushed into the room and killed the few Dura who had fled there.

The Vela were confused and frightened by the events of the night and some were reluctant to go with their liberators, thinking they were simply being taken hostage.

"If you want to live free you must come with us," were the only words they heard from any of the New Confederates.

As they headed toward the door in the east wall, Hans watched carefully. He knew all too well the danger of assuming there was no longer any threat. Even though the attack had been quick and effective, there was no guarantee some Rasset or Dura had not fled into hiding and were waiting to strike from ambush. Just as he was about to exit the compound, Hans sensed, more than saw, movement as the light from the explosions had almost totally disappeared and the night was quickly returning to total darkness. Moving quickly back instead of continuing forward, Hans felt the rush of an arrow pass where he would have been had he not reversed his direction. Standing totally still, he had to wait only a few moments until the attacker came to make certain of his kill. Hans lifted his sword and, as the attacker knelt looking for the body he was certain would be there so he could deliver the killing blow, Hans brought the sword down with such force that part of the shoulder was severed along with the arm of the would be defender of the Compound. Hans then moved out quickly and joined the rest of his group.

* * *

Similar scenes were being played out in each of the Zones. In the Red Zone Hanta's double-bladed axe severed the head or torso of many Dura; in the Yellow Zone Hazcra's mace shattered Rasset and Dura skulls alike; in the Green Zone Haisa's scimitar sliced through the bodies of any who got in his way. Accebe, Acir, Ahona, and Ahe all had opportunity to send arrows into the body of any who fled.

In the Blue Zone Neliv's sons fought with a fierceness that made him proud of their tribal heritage while he shot arrows into the body of any Rasset who came within range of his crossbow.

In the Black Zone, during the height of the battle, Niltof noticed a figure darting around the sky sleds inside the Compound. One who was not wearing a purple robe. As Niltof watched, he saw the figure harness one neox to it and lead it outside the Compound. Taking careful aim with his crossbow, Niltof let the shaft fly just as the figure vaulted into the sled. It was that movement that saved the fleeing figure's life, for the arrow intended for his torso went into and through the calf of his leg. The neox, not liking the noise of battle and the smell of fresh blood, flew quickly into the darkness and the sled was lost from sight.

CHAPTER ELEVEN

Raica awoke suddenly to the sound of running feet in the corridor outside her quarters. Quickly slipping on her covering, she sped to the door and opened it only to hear loud noises from the direction of the meeting room.

As she headed in that direction she was joined by the three Olo who had also been awakened.

"What's going on?" Sasice asked.

"I don't know—yet," was the icy reply. "Wait in your quarters while I find out."

Suddenly they all heard the thunderous voice of the Leader, "What do you mean 'attacked'? Who would dare do such a thing to us? Don't they know that to break the Treaty means we will have to punish them and the Vela will all die?"

As Raica entered the room she found Hepnet surrounded by all six of the Retona and the Leader.

He returned without reporting to me first? Raica thought. *How dare he?*

"My lords," he began, the usual grin missing from his face, "only the gods themselves kept me from being killed myself."

"Tell us exactly what happened."

"It was after moonset. There was an explosion and men ran to investigate. Then there was another explosion from the opposite end of the Compound. The next thing we knew there were men entering through openings the explosions had created. Fighting broke out everywhere."

"What was the outcome?"

"I don't know. I knew you would want to hear about the attack so I got a sky sled ready and managed to escape."

"Your wound is not from fighting then?" a Retona asked sarcastically.

Not noticing the sarcasm, Hepnet lied, "Yes, I fought valiantly until I was injured. Then I decided, since I could not fight any longer, I should report to you."

"So you do not know if the attackers were defeated or not?"

"No. Not for certain."

"Then what use is your report?" asked the sarcastic Retona.

"When I left, the attackers were releasing the Vela. I dared stay no longer lest I be killed as well and you would have no knowledge of the attacks."

"If they attacked one Compound successfully, they will try to attack the others," the Leader stated. "We must quickly make plans to fortify the other Compounds before that can occur."

"My lords," Raica said in her meekest voice, "please allow me to speak."

"What do you wish to say?" the Leader snapped.

"I believe you need to prepare for an attack here as well."

"That is ridiculous," one of the Retona stated. "They do not know about this island and could not find it even if they did."

Aware the Olo had followed her there, Raica went on to say, "the gods have revealed to me that someone has been on this island already."

Now that she had their full attention, she continued. "Someone has been here and taken an Olo captive." Although she did not know this for certain, Raica was fairly confident that was what had happened to Reke.

Enjoying being able to make the Rasset look foolish, she continued, "has anyone seen Reke, the Olo you sent to find a sero several days ago? I found the sero, right where Reke had tied it, but there was no sign of him. The gods have revealed to me that someone took him captive."

"Who could do such a thing, and why?" the Leader asked.

"The gods did not reveal who, and as for why, it should be obvious—to learn all they can about this island."

"Then we must find out if they are still here."

"I do not believe they are, but they will undoubtedly return."

"We must know immediately if they return."

"Leave that to me," Raica said with a cold smile on her lips. "I will find out and let you know the moment it happens." She was thoroughly enjoying having the Rasset need her.

Ignoring Hepnet, she turned and left the room with the Olo following behind.

* * *

Raica led the three Olo straight to their own quarters. As soon as the door closed she said, "This is your opportunity to please both the Rasset and the gods."

"What can we do?" Rahete asked eagerly. "We will do anything to put an end to the anger of the gods."

"I will tell you now because you need to know, it is the will of the gods for the Rasset to establish control over the Merene and prepare for me to take over. But someone is trying to destroy all the good the Rasset are doing."

"Why would anyone want to do such a thing?" Sasice asked.

"They desire to put an end to orderly government and allow chaos to ruin the land. There is reason to believe some of these troublemakers are on this island. I want each of you to try to find them."

"Why don't you simply ask the gods where they are?" Elacha asked sullenly.

Raica turned a withering glare at her and replied in an ice cold voice, "Because they are testing us to see if we truly want their favor. I would suggest that *you* try particularly hard since it is your rebellious spirit that has caused their disfavor."

"Elacha, please," Rahete pleaded, "please do not further anger the gods. We must do all we can to appease them or terrible things may befall us."

Raica smiled. "As quickly as you can, I want each of you to get two days provisions. Elacha, you go to the western shore and then travel north; Rahete, you go to the eastern shore and do the same; and Sasice, you head north right up the center of the island. Now hurry. Put your traveling shoes on and get started. If you find anything at all, report it to me immediately," Raica said, stressing the last two words.

* * *

Morning found one group of New Confederates in each of the Zones gathered together far enough away from the Compound not to attract any attention should there be any organized pursuit. Thankfully Haisa's signal jamming had worked, enabling the removal of the Vela from the Compounds without any deaths. Now, skilled medical men, like Hanta, were busy removing the discs from the shoulders of each Vela and taking care of any New Confederates who had been wounded during the battle.

The other five groups in each Zone were concealed, but alert for any sign of pursuit. In each Zone two men had been left behind to watch for any injured New Confederate. By midday all of them had rejoined their group. Three of them each brought an injured fighter back with them. The attackers in the Blue Zone had lost the most men. Six had been killed and twelve were wounded. The other Zones had only lost two or three men each but no loss was taken lightly. Every life was a friend, a family member, an individual who valued freedom and was willing to risk their life to gain that freedom—for others as well as themselves.

In the Blue Zone there was the greatest sorrow because Neliv, who had been the rear guard for the escaping Vela, had been killed by an arrow fired by a wounded Dura who had paid for his action with his own life when Neliv's sons quickly avenged their father's death.

As the groups prepared to disperse, each Vela was given a covering the color for the Zone they were in. Then each fighter took at least one Vela with them and returned to their Underground. The leaders of each group, and the five surviving Zone leaders all made their way back to the Blue Zone Underground to meet with the Council and report.

* * *

"The Council must meet with the Resistance right away," Vadi informed the room full of those who had returned from the destruction of the Compounds. "A few of them know the type of government we want to set up and are in full support of it, but we need to bring the rest of them on board. We must move fast before the Rasset can regroup and strike back."

"For that very reason," Hans said as he stood up to address the assembly, "I would ask the Council to allow me to go to Mystery Island once more in order to prevent them from organizing any attack or defense."

"Do you think that's wise?" Niltof asked. "The Cibth who has sworn to destroy you is on that island."

"I know. I also know that if we do not strike while the Rasset are in disarray we will not have another opportunity."

"What can one man do against all who are on the island?" Yamam asked. "We do not want to lose you."

"I will take my sons with me."

"And me," Ahe said as she stood up beside him.

"We will all go with you," one of the freedom fighters said as he rose to his feet. "We have fought together for a common goal, and we are willing to continue fighting until the last battle has been won."

All in the room voiced their agreement.

Hans stood silent for a few moments before he replied. "You cannot know how honored I am that you all feel that way," his voice choking with emotion. "However, a large force would be easily noticed and hard to conceal. Although I would be proud to fight side by side with you once more, I must ask that you allow me to take only a few with me. I thought of taking my sons because we have fought battles together before—and we are Diwesh."

"But even with your sons along you will be heavily outnumbered," Kye stated.

"Eleven of us will go."

Everyone turned to see who had just spoken with such a calm, yet authoritative voice. Areboh and Arabella stood in the doorway.

"We are all either Diwesh or married to Diwesh, with the exception of Arabella who has asked to be allowed to join us," Areboh explained as she and Arabella made their way to stand beside Hans and Ahe.

Hazcra, Hanta, Haisa, Accebe, Acir, and Ahona also joined the small group as Niltof made his way down the steps from the raised area where the Council was seated. It was difficult because of his damaged knee, but he came and stood proudly with the rest of Hans' family.

"Although we are not Merene ourselves," Hans stated, "we have been accepted and protected by you and would consider it an honor to be allowed to undertake this mission on your behalf."

"You, of all people, know the danger of such an undertaking," Vadi stated.

"Yes, we do," Hans replied, "and should we fail we ask only two things."

"Which are?" Yamam asked.

"First, that you prepare to repel the attack they will mount against you if we cannot stop them in time."

"And?"

"Second, if we should fall in battle, place our bodies upon a ship and set it out to sea and burn it. The Diwesh consider such a funeral an honor for those who fight and die valiantly."

The Council huddled together for a few moments before Vadi turned and said, "Your request to be allowed to go to Mystery Island is granted, as is your request that we be prepared in case of an attack. As for your final request—we will pray to Nido we never need honor that request."

"Thank you. We will leave at daybreak."

* * *

With Hans leading the way, the eleven made their way across the sea in three dugouts and landed at the northern end of the island. Before leaving the mainland, Hans had shown them the map he had drawn on his first visit and discussed details of Mystery Island. After landing, Hans began to make his way toward the southern end and the Settlement to learn if the Rasset knew what had happened on the mainland and, if so, what preparations they were making. The others paired off and headed for a spot Hans had told them of, each pair taking a different route.

* * *

"There are strangers on our island," one of the Rasset announced as he entered the main room.

"Where?" Sona, one of the Retona, demanded. He was a large man whose head seemed to be attached to his shoulders without any neck and was always thrust out ahead of his body. He did not have the usual commanding appearance of a Retona. His greasy, dark hair added to the overall impression of slovenliness, but the Rasset had made him a Retona and he did all he could to make certain everyone knew he was, indeed, a Retona of the powerful Rasset.

"On the northern end. I spotted them from the sky sled as I was making my morning circuit of the island."

"Where are they now?" Sona demanded.

"They scattered out in different directions. I could not tell where they were heading."

"We need to find out what they plan on doing. Send the Olo to find them. We will reward any who discover their whereabouts."

"Consider it done. The Olo are already searching for them," Raica said as she walked into the room. "And, unlike you, I am not a bumbling fool who will let them escape once they are caught."

Sona looked around the room nervously. He did not miss the sarcasm in her voice and did not want any other Rasset to hear how disrespectfully he allowed this Cibth to speak to him.

The Leader turned to look at this Cibth who dared speak without permission. Suddenly he smiled. "It seems you do have everything under control."

"I suspect the intruders are led by one I wish to see totally destroyed," she replied coldly. "If I am right, I want to be allowed to inflict limitless pain upon him."

"Assist us and, if you are correct, he will be yours to do with as you wish."

A chill went down the spine of the Leader as he saw the evil smile that spread upon the usually expressionless face of the Cibth. He had heard of the viciousness of the Cibth, but had never really believed the stories could be true. Now he was not certain.

* * *

Hans stopped suddenly. There in the path ahead was an Olo and she was alone. She seemed to be looking for something. He watched her until he was certain no one else was around. Only then did he step from concealment.

"Did you lose something?" he asked.

Startled, Sasice jumped and turned to face him.

"No. I heard there were strangers on the island and I was hoping to find them."

"Why?" he asked suspiciously.

"Because I want to help them," she lied.

"Why would you want to help them? Aren't you working for the Rasset?"

"Only because they make me. I really just want to go home."

"How did you come to be so far from the Rasset?"

"They sent me out to gather some wood for cooking"

Sasice was growing more nervous with each lie. Whoever this man was he asked entirely too many questions.

"So what happens if you don't return?"

"They will probably not care. They are much more concerned with finding the strangers and won't want to waste time looking for one Olo."

Hans was not entirely reassured but she seemed sincere.

"Come with me then. Maybe you can help us."

"I'll do whatever I can to help you against the Rasset as long as it gets me off this island."

Sasice could not help thinking how pleased Raica would be to learn that she had managed to find the strangers. Perhaps the gods would even give her a special blessing.

However, Hans did not take her to the camp where the others were located. He did not fully trust this Olo even though she seemed sincere. Instead, he headed to a concealed spot he had noted on his first visit to this island.

"We'll wait here until sunset," he explained.

"What then?"

"I must find a way to get inside the Settlement without being seen."

"What about me?"

"You will wait here until I return. Then we will meet with the others."

"What if I can show you a way in?"

"I thought you were trying to escape?"

"I am, but if I help you we can get off this island sooner can't we?"

"Yes. We cannot leave until our task is completed."

"Then as soon as the sun goes down, I will show you a way in."

Just then they heard the sound of someone else coming down the path. Sasice peered through the leaves and whispered "It's only Rahete. Stay here and I will send her on her way."

A few moments later Sasice returned. "I asked her to take the wood back for me and tell everyone I would be late because I was gathering some berries, so no one will be looking for me."

Hans was still not certain if he could totally trust this Olo, but he was willing to take a slight risk if it would help accomplish the destruction of the Rasset.

* * *

As soon as the daylight no longer illuminated the constant mist over Mystery Island, Sasice rose up and pointed to a depression behind one of the buildings in the Settlement.

"No one ever goes into that area except to feed the neox and that is done first thing in the morning. If we go around there," she pointed to the west side of the open area, "we won't be seen at all, even if someone should happen to look out one of the openings. There is a door which leads into the basement storage area."

As they slowly made their way toward the building, Hans stopped several times to scan the area and watch all the openings for any sign of activity.

When they finally arrived at their destination, Sasice opened the door and they walked down a dark corridor.

"Wait here while I make certain no one is around," she said slipping quickly into the darkness.

Hans moved to the other side of the hallway so his exact location would be known to no one and pulled his Diwesh dagger from its sheath and waited.

After a short time, he felt a rush of cool air and, fearing a trap, he started to go back the way they had entered, only to come face to face with two Dura in the almost total darkness. Turning quickly he took only two strides before he encountered more Dura. Holding the dagger low down he thrust out and up and heard a scream of agony as warm blood flowed over his hand. As he started to push his way past the Dura, he felt a terrific blow to the back of his head and fell to the floor unconscious.

* * *

When he awoke, Hans found himself in a room with five people, including Sasice and a Cibth.

"Did you really think I wanted to leave with your group?" Sasice asked as he opened his eyes. "I told Rahete to let them know I would be leading you in by way of the basement entrance. How stupid you must be."

"I like to believe," Hans replied, "that a person means what they say. It is unfortunate there are so many who lie and deceive. You must get along well with the Rasset."

"I only wish I could tell them where the rest of your group is," she said smugly. "Raica has assured me that the gods will smile upon me for my cunning."

"There is only one god you poor deluded child. And he does not reward liars and deceivers."

"Shut up!" snapped the Cibth. "You cannot speak against the gods. Do not open your mouth unless you are granted permission to speak."

"So, a Cibth is now speaking for the Rasset?" he asked, turning his attention to her.

"No one speaks for us," the Leader said ignoring the glare from Raica.

"But my lord," Hepnet said with his usual wide grin upon his face, "certainly you do not want this Reth to speak without first showing proper respect for your lordship?"

"Of course not," was the curt reply. "Nor do we need a Cibth to speak for us. She may be your wife, but she is not a Rasset."

"Of course not my lord," Hepnet replied.

Hans had not seen Hepnet for two years but there was no mistaking his traitorous offspring.

"I meant no disrespect," Raica said meekly even though she was seething inside. *This is not the time to upset them,* she thought. *After they have defeated the rebels will be the time.* "Please forgive my outspokenness. I was simply upset to see the Rasset treated with such disrespect."

As usual, Hans had been taking in his surroundings and watching everyone carefully during this whole exchange. He noticed they were all standing in front of a large window opening and there were no other buildings between the one he was in and the forested area surrounding the Settlement area. Realizing they were all watching each other and not him, he formed his hand into a fist and rose up suddenly. Before anyone knew what was happening, he smashed his fist into Hepnet's grinning mouth with such force that two teeth were broken. Continuing his momentum, he jumped over the fallen Hepnet, who was screaming in pain, and leapt through the opening. Landing on the soft ground below, he rolled over twice before coming to his feet and sprinted toward the nearby trees. He immediately disappeared into the darkness. It all happened so quickly no one had time to react. He did hear the whiz of an arrow pass by him just before he reached the trees.

* * *

Hans did not stop until he was well away from the Settlement and certain there was no pursuit. He found his way to where he had hidden his sword and continued travelling north until the moon set and the night became too dark to travel further. Finding a brallem bush, he covered himself with a few fallen leaves from the bush and slept until the first rays of daylight filtered through the mist. Hans rose, took a quick drink of water from the leaves and made his way back to the rendezvous because he knew the others would be concerned about him.

Areboh ran to greet him as soon as he entered the camp.

"I was beginning to worry," she told him.

"I had a little difficulty," he replied, "and I saw Hepnet."

"Then he is involved?"

"I am afraid so."

"He always thought he could outsmart everyone and now he is joined to a Cibth. I was hoping the report we had received was wrong."

"It wasn't," Hans replied sadly as he accepted the bowl of stew she handed him.

CHAPTER TWELVE

After telling the others about the events of the previous day, Hans gave them a detailed explanation of the layout of the Settlement. They spent the remainder of the day discussing ways of attack. With the exception of Arabella, each member of the party contributed their ideas and allowed the others to find any flaws there might be in each proposal. By nightfall they had arrived at what they all believed would be the best method.

Sunrise the next day found them moving out by five different routes. Niltof and Accebe went by one of the western routes, Hazcra and Acir by the other. Hanta and Ahona took one of the eastern routes while Haisa, Areboh, and Arabella took the other. Hans and Ahe took the center route.

* * *

"Stay here," Areboh said to Arabella, "while Haisa and I check the area ahead."

They had only been gone a short time when Arabella heard the sound of someone moving nearby. Seeking to avoid being seen, she moved away from the sound but in so doing she made noise herself. Suddenly a strong hand closed around her arm and she was dragged into the open.

"I thought I had seen someone in this area," Elacha cried.

"Hepnet, take her to the Settlement," the Cibth commanded. "We will learn all that she can tell us soon enough."

As the little procession made their way to the buildings, Areboh and Haisa watched. They had almost returned to Arabella's position when they had spotted the trio closing in on her.

"What can we do?" Areboh asked her son.

"Nothing right now. Let's just follow and watch for an opportunity."

"I have gotten to like that young woman."

"You like *all* those who are in need of help. That's what everyone loves about you."

"Blame it on my maternal instinct," she replied.

Careful not to be seen themselves, they followed and, when the trio entered one of the buildings with their prisoner in tow, Haisa and Areboh were able to find a position where they could watch the numerous window openings.

"There," Haisa whispered. "They just entered a room near the end of the building."

The sky was continuing to grow darker as the sun was setting so Areboh knew which room he was referring to when the light of a freshly lit candle began to provide illumination.

"It is almost time to meet with the others," Haisa said to his mother, "You stay here while I go to the rendezvous. They need to know what has happened."

"Don't worry. I am not going anywhere while that Cibth has Arabella in her clutches!"

Haisa quickly slipped away, anxious to report and be able to get back in case Areboh needed help. Although, judging from the sound of her voice, he was fairly certain if anyone was going to need help it would be Arabella's captors.

* * *

Ahe stood motionless as six figures walked down the path between two buildings. She had been watching the area for some time now, trying to determine just how many Rasset there were on the island.

"So, the Cibth and her Olo found one of the spies did they?"

"Yes, Leader. She has promised to learn all she can from her and report directly to you," Hepnet replied. He was glad Raica had been the one to take a prisoner. He knew she would show no mercy in obtaining information from the girl and, once she had that information and shared it with the Rasset, his position within their ranks would be secured. He smiled as he thought how they would no longer look down on him. He would truly be one of the Rasset at last.

"Good," the Leader continued, "the others are already assembled in the meeting room. I will give you the privilege of sharing the news with them."

"Thank you, my lord," Hepnet replied, his chest almost bursting with pride.

As soon as they had entered the building, Ahe stepped away from her place of concealment and headed for the rendezvous. She and Haisa arrived at almost the same time.

"Arabella is in trouble," she began, "and the Rasset are all meeting now."

"And I know where they are holding her," Haisa added. He then proceeded to fill them in on all that had transpired.

When he was finished, Hans stroked his beard slowly—a habit he had when he needed to make a decision quickly.

"Accebe, Acir, Ahona, and Ahe, you four go and help Areboh. I do not believe you will have much time. Arabella is in the hands of a Cibth. The boys and I will take care of the Rasset."

Without a moment's delay the four women took up their bows and quivers and melted soundlessly into the growing darkness.

Hans looked at the men. "So much for our plans. We will have to improvise as we go."

"Sometimes that is for the best," Niltof said as they all picked up their weapons and headed south toward the Settlement.

"Hardly seems fair," Hazcra said as they made their way by moonlight. "There are only about twenty-five of them to the five of us."

Hans almost smiled as he replied, "Just because there are not more of them to worry about, don't become careless. They will undoubtedly be in the main meeting room. There are three window openings and two doorways in that room. Niltof, I want you to go to that rise over there," he said indicating a slightly elevated position. "From there you should have a good field of fire into the room with your crossbow. Hanta and Hazcra will be ready to enter by one of the openings and Haisa and I will enter through the other. Give us a few moments to get into position and then begin shooting arrows into the room. That should draw their attention away from the other openings and allow us a few moments to enter the room. Remember, we are outnumbered, so we must attack quickly and effectively."

"Take this with you," Hazcra said as he handed Niltof his own crossbow. "You might not have time to reload right away so, once you have emptied your own crossbow you can pick this one up and keep shooting. Besides," he grinned, "I won't need it in close combat."

"Good idea," Hanta said. "Once we enter the room their attention will be divided and you should be able to get a few more."

"You all know I hate to waste arrows so I'll be making every shot count. If I can't make a kill, I will still put a real hurt on any who give me a good target." Niltof stated.

"Hans," Hazcra said, "let me make our entrance a little easier. As soon as Niltof starts shooting, I will put a match to this little packet I have and toss it into the room. The smoke it will produce will add to the confusion and we won't be able to be spotted as easily."

"Good. It will help, but we will still need to hurry if we want to block any possible escape. Once we are inside you and Haisa move to block the doorways. Hanta and I will block any escape to the outside except for the opening the arrows will be coming through."

The four Diwesh moved to positions under the other two openings into the room and waited. They did not need to wait for long. Suddenly from within the room they heard startled shouts and sudden movement. Hazcra lit and tossed his packet into the center of the room filling it with thick, black smoke. The Diwesh immediately grabbed the ledge and pulled themselves up and soundlessly dropped to the floor inside. Haisa and Hazcra sprinted to block the doorways and Haisa let the scuzzets out of their traveling bag. All four men pulled their weapons from their sheaths and let out a loud whoop which caused the Rasset to turn. As they did, they were met with an onslaught of metal. Scimitar, axe, mace, and broadsword swung into unprotected bodies. The attack was so sudden and unexpected that the Rasset lost precious moments of reaction time. Before they could comprehend what was happening, the battle was fully upon them. Hans swung his broadsword with such force that it sliced through both the knees of one Dura and the thigh of a Rasset; Hanta's double bladed axe removed the heads of two Dura; Haisa's scimitar sliced through the bellies of two Retona and his Diwesh dagger swung back and left a long, bloody gash in the upper arm of a Rasset. Hazcra's mace smashed the side of one Rasset's head and the face of another while his Diwesh dagger swung to prevent anyone from approaching him from behind. Niltof's arrows pierced the bodies of two Rasset and two Dura, wounding the Rasset and killing the Dura.

The scuzzets quickly ran from one Rasset to another. Too quick to be caught or killed, their continual attack added to the confusion with their unexpected biting of some and clawing of others. Keeping only enough space between them to allow free use of the weapons, the Diwesh formed an arc and advanced upon the Rasset. Although the smoke was quickly dissipating, they still had the advantage of knowing where each of the others were so they could use their weapons without fear of hurting anyone except their enemies. The Diwesh began pushing the Rasset back toward the opening which continued to be pierced by occasional arrows.

Not expecting any immediate attack, the Rasset and Retona had only their daggers with which to fight. Although the Dura were armed, there were only ten of them and five were out of action within moments after the attack began.

One of the Rasset tried to slip around the end of the Diwesh arc and was about to strike Haisa from behind when there was a blur of green and brown. He fell, screaming, to the floor as both scuzzets leapt upon him and began tearing at his face with their teeth and claws.

Hepnet was one of the first to draw his dagger and prepare to fight but as he turned to face the attackers he saw Hans and all the bravado left him. He, better than any of the others, knew the courage and determination of this man and those fighting alongside him for he was the traitorous son who had betrayed his own father. Panic swept over him like a wave of ice cold water and, as the smoke continued to thin, he began to look for a way of escape. Suddenly he felt a strong hand grasp the wrist holding his dagger and force it behind him.

"Drop the weapon," a soft voice said, "and my dagger will not pierce your rotten body."

He recognized Hazcra's voice and knew the threat was not an idle one. As he let his own Diwesh dagger fall from his grasp, he saw the Leader's bloody body fall to the floor. As suddenly as it had begun, the battle was over. Looking around the room, all Hepnet saw was blood and the dead bodies of the proud Rasset littering the floor. He was the only one to survive and he knew it was *not* because of his fighting skill. He was a captive who had been spared solely because of his father.

As Hans and the other two brothers approached Hepnet he heard the familiar voice of Niltof.

"I think I really like this new crossbow," he said as he lifted himself over the sill of the opening. "After the fighting inside started I began coming closer. Three of them tried to jump through this opening but they made much too good a target to pass up."

"Are there any others elsewhere?" Hanta asked as Hazcra pushed the point of his dagger just enough for Hepnet to feel the pressure.

"No," was the surly reply, "there are only Olo left."

"And your Cibth," Haisa said disgustedly.

"What do we do with this traitorous coward who shames our family and the name of Diwesh?" Hazcra asked.

"A weakling who hides behind women and flees from a fight," Niltof added.

"He is still my son—even if it is by blood only," Hans stated, "and I mourn the day of his birth. However, I will not allow any of my family to take the life of family."

"I have an idea," Niltof stated. "What is it that allows everyone to know a Diwesh?"

"That's easy," Haisa replied. "It is the fact that our eyes are two different colors—one green and the other blue."

"That's right. All other races have two eyes the same color and none of them have blue eyes."

"So?" Haisa asked.

"So, if Hepnet did not have a blue eye no one would ever know he was born a Diwesh."

"It seems fitting," Hazcra stated. "He wanted nothing to do with us and betrayed our father into the hands of his enemies. Let his traitorous heart cost him his blue eye. Without it, no one will believe him if he should ever claim to be Diwesh."

The others all nodded their approval and looked at Hans who, after several moments of silence, said, "It is a fitting punishment, but I, as his father, must administer it since I am responsible for bringing this evil into the world."

Without any further words, the solemn group made its way outside and headed toward the rendezvous spot. Upon arriving, Hanta and Haisa built a small fire. As Hans began to heat Hepnet's own dagger over the fire, Hepnet broke the silence.

"You cannot really do this," he exclaimed in disbelief. "I am your own son!"

"No," Hans said softly. "You *were* my son. However, being a son is much more than an accident of birth. A true son honors his father—even if he is imperfect—and stands by and protects the family. You have done just the opposite. You sought to have me killed and endangered the entire family. I regret being responsible for bringing you into the world."

When Hans rose from the fire, eight strong hands took hold of Hepnet's body, holding it perfectly still. Suddenly the quiet of the night was shattered by a blood curdling scream.

As the other three sons faded into the night to be alone with their sorrow and find their women, Niltof helped Hans put salve and a bandage over the eye and pretended he did not notice the tear making its way down Hans' cheek.

* * *

It took only moments for Accebe, Acir, Ahona, and Ahe to find Areboh who was now crouched beneath a window opening into the room where Arabella was being held.

"I am afraid the Cibth is losing patience," she whispered as the four girls came up alongside her.

"I will only ask you one more time," they all heard the Cibth say in a shrill voice, "where are the others and how many are there?"

"I have nothing to say to anyone who works for the Rasset," Arabella replied calmly but firmly.

Areboh moved to the side of the opening. She was just tall enough to be able to look into the room. Arabella was in the middle of it, facing toward the window opening, seated upon a low stool so the short Cibth did not have to look up to her prisoner. The Cibth and three Olo were facing their captive.

"Do you not realize I have the power to do to you whatever I wish?" Raica asked as she moved closer and slapped her as hard as she could. Areboh saw Arabella's head turn sharply from the force of the blow.

Seeing no fear in the eyes of her captive, she looked at the Olo and said, "I will teach this wench not to defy a Cibth or refuse to answer my questions."

As she spoke she drew a short curved knife from the gold amulet she wore around her neck and cut a long gash across Arabella's cheek.

Areboh saw her clench her teeth to keep from crying out in pain. The Olo all seemed fascinated by the whole proceedings and stood motionless.

Moving even closer to her prisoner, Raica placed the knife under Arabella's chin, using the feel of the metal to force her to look into the Cibth's cold, dark eyes. As the blood flowed down her cheek, Arabella glared at her tormentor defiantly.

"Now," the Cibth said more calmly, "where are they?"

"Why do you waste time?" Elacha asked. "This one is not going to tell you anything."

Seeing that the Cibth and Olo were totally focused on Arabella, Areboh pulled herself up onto the sill of the opening and quietly dropped to the floor inside. Moving quickly, she made her way to a dark corner of the candle lit room and stood motionless. Seeing Areboh disappear into the room, Accebe and Ahe pulled themselves up, cast a quick look around the room, and moved to the other corner. Acir and Ahona immediately followed them onto the sill of the opening and dropped soundlessly to the floor below, where they remained crouched in the shadows. Although Arabella noticed these last two enter, she did not change her expression in the least.

"You, of all people," Raica responded to Elacha's question, "should know how difficult it can be to make a stubborn one talk. I have some special ways to persuade such a one to tell me all I want to know," she stated as she looked down at her captive and slid the flat side of the knife under Arabella's chin and laughed.

"I think it's time for you to stop now," Areboh spoke from the darkness.

Raica whirled, her eyes flashing anger at this unexpected interruption.

As Areboh stepped from the darkness, Raica quickly moved behind Arabella, keeping her between this intruder and herself.

"Cut her loose and you can live," Areboh said as she drew her Diwesh dagger from its sheath.

"You," she said motioning to one of the Olo, "take the knife from this Cibth and cut the girl loose."

"And if I don't?" the Olo asked defiantly.

"If you don't, I will throw you out into the darkness." She knew the threat was not wasted on the superstitious Olo by the widening eyes and nervous glances into the darkness outside.

Raica stood motionless as the Olo moved toward her to do as Areboh had commanded. Just as Elacha reached for the knife, Raica thrust it deep into Arabella's back and gave it a violent twist.

"You fiend," Areboh screamed as she sprang across the room and knocked the short Cibth to the floor with a blow made more powerful by her anger. All three of the Olo fled from the room and Ahe, Accebe, and Acir ran after them. Ahona stayed behind to help Areboh.

Rushing to Arabella, Areboh needed only a glance to know she had not suffered at all. The thrust had been unexpected and deadly. Ahona had moved swiftly to prevent the Cibth from escaping. Any intention of trying to flee left the Cibth as she saw the razor sharp dagger in the hands of her opponent and the look of determination on her face.

Turning her attention to the Cibth, Areboh felt an anger building up inside her such as she had never experienced before. Arabella had done nothing to harm anyone. She had suffered at the hands of the Rasset, and now her life had been taken by a bitter, evil, conniving Cibth for no real reason at all.

"What is *wrong* with you?" she asked Raica. "What did you think such an act would accomplish?"

"Don't blame me," Raica said defiantly. "If you had not interfered she might still be alive."

"She lies," Ahona said. "We all saw what she was doing, and what she intended to do."

"You had better be careful how you treat me," Raica continued. "The gods listen very well to what I tell them."

"Do you think we are as stupid as your Olo pawns?" Areboh said in amazement. "There is only one god and I assure you he has nothing to do with you and your plans. You use your false gods to suit your own purposes and control those foolish enough to believe they exist and you can influence them."

"There *are* many gods," the Cibth insisted loudly, "and they hear and answer my prayers."

"Then I recommend you quickly petition them. I have not yet decided what to do with you, but granting you a long life is *not* one of the things I am considering."

Hoping to create doubt in the minds of these two women, Raica wrapped her hand around her amulet and began to chant in a strange language.

After allowing her to drone on for several minutes, Areboh snapped, "Enough!"

"Ahona, hold her arms."

Before she could react, Raica's arms were held securely behind her back.

"Much as I would like to, I will not take even your worthless life," Areboh stated.

Raica felt the fear she had been experiencing begin to leave her body.

"However, I believe your gods must be as tired of your chattering and lies as I am, so I will do them, and everyone else, a favor."

Before the Cibth could comprehend what was happening, Areboh reached out, grabbed hold of her tongue, pulled it out as far as she could, and used her keen Diwesh dagger to slice clean through it.

As she felt her mouth fill with blood, Raica stared at Areboh in disbelief. She futilely tried to utter curses at her foe but only garbled sounds came out. She screamed, almost choking on her own blood, as Areboh tossed the severed piece out the window opening.

Without giving the Cibth a backward glance, the two women left the room to find the rest of their party.

CHAPTER THIRTEEN

Each of the Olo ran in a different direction upon fleeing the room. Accebe, the first to exit the room, caught a glimpse of Rahete heading down the south corridor and ran after her. Ahe was only a moment behind her sister and spotted Sasice heading down the northern corridor and gave chase. Acir, the last to leave the room, was certain Elacha had gone down the central corridor and set out to find her.

* * *

Rahete came to the end of the corridor and passed through a door which opened upon the narrow bridge joining the living quarters to the armory. Wanting to avoid getting involved in any fighting, she began walking rapidly across the bridge hoping to hide until morning. Accebe ran down the corridor and burst through the door. Spotting the fleeing Olo, she demanded, "Stop right where you are," and drew back on the bow in her hand.

Rahete halted and turned to face her pursuer.

"What is your name?" Accebe demanded. "So I may know what to put on your grave marker."

"I am called Rahete," she replied, "and I have done nothing to harm you. Let me be on my way. I am only a bystander."

"Rahete, you are the one who had an opportunity to warn Hans he was walking into a trap. Why didn't you?"

"It was none of my concern."

"But you knew they sought to kill him."

"Listen, I only want to go my own way. I want nothing to do with this fight or any other. Now let me be on my way."

"Go your way," Accebe said as she took the tension off the bowstring and lowered her weapon. "I will not waste an arrow on such a coward as you."

Furious at the delay, and fearful it might have endangered her chance to escape, Rahete spun around and began to run across the narrow bridge. Suddenly her foot slipped on a loose stone and she fell screaming, and landed, a crumpled mass, on the ground below.

Accebe turned and headed back the way she had come.

* * *

As she spotted Sasice going down the northern corridor, Ahe sprinted as fast as she could to catch up to the Olo. Coming to a cross corridor, she looked both ways and almost missed seeing the back of the Olo slip into a room. Not wanting her quarry to escape, she ran to the door and, with her bow in one hand, cautiously opened the door. She found the room was empty except for the Olo who was trying to hide in a corner.

"Come out and tell me your name," Ahe demanded, "and I might allow you to live. If you remain where you are I will send an arrow into your cowardly heart." As she spoke she drew an arrow from her quiver, fit it to the bow, and pulled back on the bowstring.

Slowly, cautiously, the Olo came out of the corner.

"My name is Sasice."

"You!" Ahe exclaimed as she kept the crossbow aimed at the Olo. "I am glad it was I who found you."

"Why?" Sasice asked, her eyes flashing her hatred at being caught.

"Because you are the one who betrayed my father's trust. You told him you would never lie to him. You claimed you wanted to help us. Then you almost got him killed when you revealed to the Rasset where he was."

"Hans is your father?"

"Yes."

"He deserves to be killed," Sasice said scornfully. "He has killed innocent people—including my husband Kar."

"It is true that he once killed someone by mistake. But that was because he trusted someone who said one thing to him, and something altogether different to someone else. Besides, that was long ago and because of that one error, now even in battle he will not deliver a killing blow. As for your husband, it was my brother, Haisa, who spilled Kar's worthless entrails on the ground."

"If Hans does not enjoy killing why does he go into battle?" Sasice sneered.

"Because if good men are not willing to fight, evil men will prevail."

"You are Diwesh. What do you know about living peacefully?"

"The Diwesh are peaceful people. We do not seek violence. However, we will not allow others to rule over us. Only Nido has the right to rule us."

"So you have no government?"

"Yes, we do. But each person who serves in a governing position realizes it is a responsibility that he or she must answer to Nido for someday. Our governors do not oppress or mistreat others."

"Enough of this chatter," Sasice snapped. "What do you intend to do with me?"

"Need some help?" Haisa asked as he entered the room. "I was looking for you and heard voices."

"Actually, I just had an idea and it will require a little help. If you tie her up for me I'll do the rest."

Wasting no time, Haisa quickly had Sasice's hands tied tightly behind her back.

"Now what?" he asked.

"Well," Ahe replied as she lowered the bow, "I think we should let the world know that this Olo is two-faced. Hold her head still."

Walking up to Sasice, Ahe drew the razor-sharp Diwesh dagger from the sheath on her thigh. As Haisa held her head firmly in his powerful hands, Ahe placed the tip of the blade on Sasice's forehead at the hairline. Having helped Hanta many times she knew exactly how deep to cut without killing. She slowly drew the dagger down the forehead to the bridge of the nose then down the center of the nose until she came to the tip of it. Ahe lifted the dagger for a moment and Sasice screamed in pain.

"I would keep my mouth shut if I were you," Haisa said. "You don't want her to slip."

Ahe placed the tip of the dagger just under the Olo's nose and split the skin from there to the mouth. Then lifted the blade and began again just below the lower lip. The dagger continued its journey down to the chin, then back to where the lower jaw met the neck. There it finally stopped its journey. Although Ahe had been careful not to cut too deeply, the blood flowed and covered Sasice's chest. Ahe knew the skin would grow back in time but the line her dagger had drawn dividing Sasice's face in half would always be a scar.

"Now everyone who sees you will be warned of your two faced nature," Ahe stated with satisfaction.

"Haisa, untie her and let her go."

As soon as had freed her, Haisa and Ahe left the Olo alone in the room.

* * *

Moving rapidly down the central corridor, Acir looked for any sign of the Olo. Just as she was about to abandon her search she heard a slight rustling coming from a room she had just passed. Turning around quickly she saw a figure run down the corridor in the direction she had just come from.

Drawing an arrow from her quiver, she nocked it, drew back the bowstring and let the arrow fly. It sliced through the side of the Olo's thigh and she fell to the floor. Acir ran to the fallen victim just as Hazcra came running down the corridor.

"I see you caught one of them," he said with a smile.

"I didn't want to kill her—just in case we can find a use for a worthless Olo."

"I am not worthless," Elacha spat. "I am a worker, and I am beautiful as well. Perhaps even you desire me," she said as she looked at Hazcra.

"No thanks," Hazcra replied. "I prefer women who do not love themselves."

"Well, at least bind up the wound this awful woman gave me," she said gesturing toward Acir.

"Better watch yourself," Acir said, "or my next arrow will be through your heart."

Hazcra knelt down and examined the wound.

"You'll live," he said as he tore a strip off the Olo's covering and used it to bind the wound.

Suddenly the Olo jerked herself out of his grip, ran into the nearest room and, as he ran after her, jumped through the opening and into the darkness beyond.

"I thought all Olo were afraid of the dark," Acir said as she came up alongside her husband.

"That's what we've always been told. But I think this Olo was a little different. Besides," he continued, "I think I smelled chooll on her breath."

Chooll was a juice extracted from the gusar trees that grew in only a few locations along the southern edge of the mainland. After the juice was extracted it was mixed with the sweet grains from the center of curagena and heated. The result was a liquid which diminished pain and enabled the consumer to overcome normal fear. However, repeated consumption resulted in an inability to distinguish between right and wrong.

"That would also explain how she could run on that injured leg," Hazcra added.

"Where would an Olo get her hands on chooll?" Acir asked.

"Well, even though the Rasset are too smart to use it often, they do like to indulge in it once in awhile. They also might keep some on hand for its pain relieving properties."

"But would they ever give it to an Olo?"

"Who knows what a Rasset might do if he thought it would suit his purpose? Let's head back to the rendezvous spot. The others are either there or will be soon."

"Good idea," Acir replied, "and on the way you can tell me why there is blood all over you. I do hope none of it is your own."

Putting his arm around her, Hazcra smiled and began to tell her about the battle as they headed out to find the others.

* * *

As they approached the rendezvous area, Hazcra and Acir could see the glow of a small fire. Upon entering the clearing, they discovered all the others were already there. Hans was the first to notice them approach.

"I was beginning to wonder if the two of you needed help," he said.

"We were just cleaning up a little of the trash on this island," Hazcra replied.

Areboh brought both the latecomers a bowl of stew and asked, "Did you find your Olo?"

"Yes," Acir replied, "but after Hazcra bound her wound she jumped out of the building and ran into the darkness."

"Into the darkness?" Hans asked.

"I'm pretty certain I smelled chooll," Hazcra stated.

"That would explain it. It will be light soon. I think we should round up the Olo and decide what to do with them."

The Diwesh spent the remainder of the time until daylight sharing with one another the events of the night, treating all cuts and bruises, and discussing various ideas of what to do with the survivors. Just as the sky was beginning to grow lighter, Hazcra slapped his hand on his thigh and proclaimed, "I've got it!"

Everyone looked at him, waiting for further information.

"Hans, you said this was a man-made island right?" he asked.

"Yes. It is simply dirt piled on a metal base that is anchored to the ocean bottom. On my first visit I dove in and found one of the anchors. Why?"

"Haisa, I need you to figure out how the base was put together," Hazcra continued. "Then I can determine where to place the explosives to blow this island up. We can put the survivors on it and end their treacherous existence."

"No," Areboh said softly but firmly. "There has been enough bloodshed for now."

"Besides," Hans added, "we have fought our battle with them. We will not take a life outside of battle."

"But we can't turn them loose on the mainland," Hanta objected. "Who knows what they might try to do?"

"Well then," Ahe spoke up, "what if Hazcra planted the explosives in such a way that the island is broken into pieces with them on one of the pieces? You could do that couldn't you Hazcra?"

"It wouldn't be difficult—unless the construction is really complicated," he answered.

"You boys get busy figuring it out while the women, Niltof, and I find the survivors of last night," Hans stated as he rose from his seat and picked up his broadsword. "We will all meet in the main dining room tomorrow."

As the three boys headed out, Hans and Niltof roused the sleeping Hepnet and they all headed to the Settlement area. Leaving Niltof and Ahona in the dining room to watch over their captive, Hans and the other four set out to find the Cibth and Olos.

* * *

As they searched the space between the living quarters and the armory, Acir and Accebe found Rahete. As they examined her Accebe said, "Well, you won't be running away from anything again. Your right foot is totally shattered."

A quick search of the rooms nearby enabled them to find two poles and a blanket. Cutting strips to use as ties, they attached the blanket to the poles and formed a stretcher to carry Rahete on.

Upon entering the dining room, they learned Ahona had located some medical supplies, The three of them went to work with salves and bandages, treating the Olo's many bruises and taping the foot as best they could.

Niltof kept watch over the sullen Hepnet.

* * *

Ahe found Sasice asleep in the corner of the room where she and Haisa had left her.

"Get up worthless one," she said.

Sasice looked at the young girl standing in the doorway with a bow and arrow in her hand. "Do you intend to take my life now?" she asked.

"No, but if you try to run this arrow will become a part of your leg. Get up and we will join the others in the dining room."

"I don't want anyone to see me like this," she protested.

"Don't worry. Everyone already knows your true nature. Now get up and let's get moving."

Reluctantly the Olo arose and walked meekly to the dining room. They arrived just as Accebe, Acir, and Ahona were finishing their work on Rahete.

"Another patient," Accebe said.

Ahona turned to look and stifled the gasp which almost escaped when she say the blood crusted line down Sasice's face. The three of them began cleaning her up and applying salve and bandages.

* * *

Hans looked for the runaway Olo and found her a short distance from where she had exited the building. Her hair was entangled in the branches of a rohn bush and her face was badly scratched. Rohn bushes had delicious berries, but they were difficult to obtain because of the abundant thorns which grew to be an inch or more in length.

"What happened to you?" Hans asked as he approached.

"I was running away and I guess the branches scratched me. I don't know because I didn't feel anything at the time. Then I got all tangled up in this stupid bush and now I hurt all over."

"Well, some of those scratches are going to leave permanent scars," he said after examining the situation, "and it looks like the only way to get you loose is to cut all the hair that is tangled." With that he drew his dagger and began cutting.

"My hair, my beautiful hair," the Olo cried, weeping as more and more hair was cut.

As soon as she was free, Hans escorted her to the dining room where Acir, Ahona, and Accebe began tending to her while Ahe helped Niltof keep an eye on those who had already been treated.

"Has anyone seen Areboh?" Hans asked while the girls worked with salve and bandages.

"No, but I can show you where the Cibth was left," Ahe offered.

"Come with me then. Niltof can keep things under control here. She is looking for the most dangerous one of the bunch."

Picking up her bow and quiver, Ahe left the building with her father.

* * *

Ahe led Hans straight to the room where the Cibth had held Arabella captive. A quick look around revealed Areboh had taken time to cover the body of the ex-Vela before going after the Cibth. Leaving the room by the window opening they quickly found Areboh following a trail.

"She left the building and headed northeast," Areboh said. "I found her trail and have been following it. Where do you suppose she's going?"

"Who can tell the mind of a Cibth?" Hans replied. "You keep following the trail. Ahe and I will be a short distance away on either side."

Hans soon noticed they were traveling in an arc and heading back toward the Settlement. "Keep going," he said in a low voice. "I have a hunch where she is heading. The two of you continue to follow the trail in case I am wrong. I will run on ahead to where I think the trail will take us. If I am right it is imperative that I get there before she does."

With that said, he began moving rapidly toward the buildings. If his suspicions were correct he could not allow the Cibth to arrive ahead of him.

He saw the Cibth and the door of the armory at the same time and began running. Raica heard the noise and turned to see who was approaching. That moment's delay allowed Hans to jump in front of the door and prevent her from entering.

"Going somewhere?" he panted.

She looked at him with hatred evident in every fiber of her being. As she turned to run away she came face to face with Ahe who had followed close behind her father. Standing with her dagger ready, Ahe said, "Go ahead, try to run. Then I will have an excuse to end your miserable existence."

The Cibth stood motionless as Hans approached and tied her hands behind her back. As they started toward the dining room, Areboh caught up with them.

"So where was she headed and how did you know?"

"She was going to the armory. When I realized she was headed back to the Settlement I couldn't figure out why at first. Then it dawned on me. The Rasset probably have explosives stored there and, knowing how hateful a Cibth can be, I figured she intended to use them to blow all of us up—including our prisoners if need be."

Raica glared at him even more hatefully.

"Based on her reaction," Ahe said, "I would say you were correct."

As they entered the dining room Niltof smiled and said, "I always wondered what a Cibth looked like. They really aren't much are they?"

"Don't let their size fool you," Hans replied. "Like a powerful poison, a little can do a great deal of damage."

The Cibth headed straight for Hepnet and began pointing and gesturing and growing more and more frustrated when it was evident he did not understand what she was trying to say to him. Finally she kicked him and, as he rose from the floor, took him by the hand and pointed to the table and made motions indicating eating.

"I think she wants him to fix her some supper," Ahona said as they all laughed at the comical scene which had just been played out before them.

"It would probably be a good idea if we all ate," Areboh said. "I'll see what I can find to fix for a meal."

"Maybe you should let Hepnet cook," Niltof said with a big grin on his face.

"I don't think I would trust his cooking," Accebe said. "He might try to add some of the Rasset's preferred delicacies or some poison. No thank you! I will help my mother cook so we can all eat without worrying."

CHAPTER FOURTEEN

"So what have you discovered?" Hans asked the three boys when they returned the next day.

"It appears the base of the island was made by joining six sections together," Haisa replied.

"And, unless I miss my guess," Hazcra added, "a few well placed explosives will break it into six separate pieces."

"I am fairly certain you will find all the explosives you need in the armory," Hans stated as the Cibth glared at him from where she was seated across the room.

"What will happen to the pieces?" Ahona asked.

"Based on what we found," Haisa said, "each piece was made separately and floated here before joining them together. If the joints are destroyed, each piece will still remain afloat. It will be a very large raft."

"Then I think we have found an answer to our problem," Hans said.

"What did you have in mind?" Areboh asked.

"We will put one of our prisoners on each piece. When the island breaks apart, each piece will be sent in a different direction. Then this troublesome quintet will no longer be together. Since they all seem to want to destroy the lives of others, let us do what we can to prevent them from having opportunity to do so again."

"But how will they live?" asked Areboh.

"Based on what we have seen, there is plenty of vegetation throughout the island and we can split the niso herd into five equal groups and put one group on each section. There will be enough food to keep someone alive—if they are willing to work. A task which may prove difficult for some, but it is possible. I believe even a Cibth can do for herself if she has no other choice."

This last comment brought another hate-filled glare from across the room.

"What about water?" Ahona asked.

"The moisture of a single brallem bush collects more than enough water to sustain a person. I believe that is why the Rasset brought so many to this island. They wanted to be able to exist here without needing any necessities from the mainland."

"Why did the Rasset build this island anyway?" Ahe asked.

"You need to realize," Hans began, "the Rasset were originally Merene themselves. They were chosen by their peers to govern what are now the Six Zones. Over time, they began to think of themselves as better than the very ones whose interests they were supposed to represent and protect. They began making laws and levying taxes for the rest of the Merene but excluding themselves. Before long, even the Merene began to consider these rulers as a higher class than themselves and the separation between rulers and the ruled grew even greater.

"Finally the Rasset decided it was time to drop any pretense and simply make themselves despots. In order to accomplish this with minimum difficulty, they began calling themselves Rasset and pretended to be a foreign power far superior to the Merene army. The Dura are the leaders of the Merene army who were included in the Rasset's plan.

"The Resistance is made up of those rulers who refused to go along with the plan. They truly wanted to protect and serve the Merene, which is why we think they will quickly join the New Confederates now that the threat of Rasset retaliation is removed. They only agreed to the treaty with the Rasset because it protected most of the Merene from enslavement and they thought they could prevent further aggression through the inspections of the Compounds.

"So if they planned on ruling over the Merene, why build this island?"

"Although they want to rule over others, the Rasset really consider themselves better than anyone else and do not like even coming in contact with others. Their plan was to live here with a minimum of Vela, who would live and eat separately, doing the work for them. The Rasset would have no contact with any Merene, or anyone else for that matter. Protected by the

Dura, served by the Vela, and imposing their will on the Merene through the Retona, the Rasset could live in what they considered paradise.

"Now you see one of the big problems with power. Few people are able to resist misusing it. Something the Diwesh learned long ago and took steps to prevent and, hopefully, something the Merene have now learned and the New Confederates can prevent. No one who rules is any better, or more important, than those he rules over. Remember that always."

"That's why our family got involved?"

"Yes. We must always be willing to help those who seek to throw off the oppressive rule of others. Yet we must also make certain there is a government, for without government there is only chaos. Men must have rules to live by to keep others—and themselves—in check. If there are no rules—no law—each person must decide what is right or wrong and they will not often agree. In a community of any kind, each person gives up a certain amount of individual freedom for the sake of the whole, but everyone—including those who make the laws—must respect the rights of everyone else.

"Now, I smell food. It is time to eat and then we have much work to do."

"Wait," Ahe said, "what about the sixth piece of the island? What will happen to it?"

"That is the one with all the buildings on it," Hanta replied.

"That one will be sunk," Hans stated.

* * *

By nightfall the explosives had been set, the niso herd divided, and Arabella's body had been placed in a hastily constructed casket.

As they gathered for a late meal Hans said "Areboh, Haisa and I will take the first watch over the prisoners. We will wake Niltof, Accebe and Ahe after two hours. Hazcra, Acir, Hanta, and Ahona will have the last watch. You will need to be very alert because they have heard all our plans and know tonight will be their last opportunity to escape. Hepnet and the Cibth are probably the greatest risk, but do not ignore the Olo."

As the others went to sleep, Hans and Areboh sat close together.

"Is it really almost over?" she asked.

"Soon. We must send these troublemakers on their way and then we can return to the mainland and there will be no more running and hiding."

"I wish there was another way."

"So do I, but you know the evil of a Cibth as well as I do. We must either exile her or take her life, and I have difficulty taking even the life of a Cibth outside of battle."

"And Hepnet and the Olo?"

"They were really nothing more than pawns in Raica's plan. Unfortunately, they joined with her and have been contaminated by her. Never again will they fit into a society where evil is not rewarded and people do not all have ulterior motives."

* * *

The night passed without incident, possibly due to the fact that during his watch Niltof had tied all five of the captives in such a way that every other one was facing the opposite direction and no one could move without all the others going the same direction.

When Hans woke and saw what had been done, he grinned the biggest grin anyone had seen on his face in a long time.

Hazcra left to set off the explosions while the others harnessed two neox to each of five sky sleds. Soon a large explosion was heard, then four others, each slightly fainter. When Hazcra returned, he was wearing the smile of one who has had a job go exactly as planned.

One captive was loaded in each sky sled along with two of the Diwesh family. Arabella's casket was placed in the sled with Hans and Areboh. As the five sky sleds rose in the air they could all see that the pieces of the island had not only been broken apart, but each one had been sent in a different direction and, by the time the momentum of the blast ended they would be miles apart.

Each sky sled took one captive to a pre-selected location on a different piece of what had been Mystery Island. They were set down and given a dagger which had been taken from the fallen Rasset.

After all five sleds had deposited their cargo and were safely in the air again, Hazcra set off the last explosion. The Diwesh circled until they were certain it sank and the other five sections all remained afloat. Only then did they turn and head for the mainland.

* * *

Not wanting anyone to think the Rasset were attacking, the five sky sleds flew over the Middle Sea and landed on the west shore of the Blue Zone just after sunset.

"The outer coasts are probably being watched closely," Hans said, "but I doubt they will be looking for any attack this far inland."

Needing to find a place to rest before moonset, they quickly found a place to hide the sleds and neox and then headed toward the east. Coming upon an abandoned dwelling, they made certain there was no sign of recent activity nearby. Then Hans and Hanta took first watch while the others wasted no time finding a place to sleep.

As the sun began to rise, everyone was awake. After taking a few moments to eat a food pouch and drink some water, they all began the journey east toward the main Underground. Not certain if everything had gone as planned, they travelled carefully.

After traveling for an hour, they suddenly heard the sound of hooves. Quickly scattering and hiding, they waited. In a few moments four riders could be seen. Hans instantly noted the riders were mounted on the swift bairan and none of them wore a covering. They were all dressed in traditional Merene garb. Dropping from the tree he had climbed, he walked toward the approaching riders. When they spotted him they slowed down and cautiously approached.

"Nido be praised," one of the men proclaimed. "It's Hans!"

Hans instantly recognized the voice of Vadi and an actual smile came upon his face.

"So, it would appear all is well here on the mainland," Hans responded.

"Couldn't be finer. We are now the Confederated Zones of Merene. The Resistance was more than willing to listen to the plans the New Confederates proposed for a new government and, even as we speak, they are drawing up the final papers of agreement for the new government. Within a month elections will be held. All the Vela have been allowed to return to their homes."

"So why aren't you there helping?"

"I am on my way to Berity right now. That's where the formal signing and celebrating will take place tomorrow. But tell me, what about the Rasset on Mystery Island? Are they a threat? When you didn't return, some feared they had defeated you and might be planning an attack, so our defenses have all been watching carefully. Wait a minute," Vadi said suddenly. "How did you get here without being spotted? We have watchers all along the coast. And where is the rest of your family?"

"We are Diwesh, remember?" Hans replied as he turned and motioned to the others. "We are cautious by nature. Therefore we did not return by a method or route which would be watched. And you need not fear the Rasset any longer."

"Come along with us. There are many who will want to hear what has happened."

"We will join you at Berity. There is something we must attend to first. Is travel free and unrestricted now?"

"Yes. But let me give you a script just in case anyone should stop you."

As Vadi dug through the pouch on the back of his bairan, Haisa approached.

"Are there still restrictions as far as what type of transportation is allowed to be used?" he asked.

"As you can see," one of the men with Vadi replied, "we are now free to travel however we please. We found these mounts near one of the destroyed Compounds and have enjoyed being able to move more rapidly."

"Then we are free to use sky sleds?" Haisa asked.

"Sky sleds?" one of the other men exclaimed. "There are none here. The Rasset had moved all of them to Mystery Island."

"That's where we got them," Haisa said.

"Traveling in them might cause some people to fear the Rasset are returning," Vadi said, "but if that is the transportation you have—by all means use it. Now tell me, what is it that prevents you from joining us right now?"

"We have an obligation we must fulfill first," Hans replied. "We must take Arabella's body to her family. They need to be able to bury her where and how they wish, and they also should know she died a hero."

"I am sorry to hear she is gone," Vadi said somberly, "but please hurry. The entire Council will want to hear your report and have you join in the celebration."

"We will be there," said Areboh who now stood beside her husband. "We wouldn't want to miss it."

As the four riders rode off, the Diwesh hurried back to where the sky sleds were hidden.

* * *

"Reda, someone's coming in sky sleds."

"Quick, run and hide. I will see what they want."

As five sky sleds approached in a "V" formation, Reda feared only the worst. Only Rasset were allowed to use them and even though he had heard they had been defeated, the sight of the sleds made him wonder.

The neox landed gracefully and came to a smooth stop a short distance from where he stood. A man and woman in strange garb stepped out of the first sled and approached him.

"You are Reda, Arabella's father?" the blonde haired man asked.

"Yes, although she was taken from us by the Rasset," he replied.

"Please get your wife, we have news about your daughter we would like to share with both of you."

Seeing his hesitation, Areboh said, "Do not worry. We are Diwesh. We have fought with the New Confederates against the Rasset."

Reda turned and called out to his wife, Dero. As she came from the house, the occupants of the other four sleds approached. Four of them were carrying a large wooden box.

"We have come to bring your daughter's body for you to bury," Hans stated. "I wish we could have brought her back to you alive. It is important for you to know she was able to escape from the Compound and she joined the New Confederates. Without her we would not have learned how soon the Rasset were planning their big move and would have missed our opportunity to defeat them. Her assistance will be recorded in your history. She may not have fought the Rasset in battle, but she was instrumental in bringing about their defeat. She died because she would not betray her friends to the Rasset and their Cibth. We would consider it an honor if you would allow us to help you lay her to rest."

As the tears welled up in his eyes and his voice choked with emotion, Reda said, "I have heard of the Diwesh and their bravery. I have heard of the New Confederates and their determination to rid our land of the Rasset. I—no we—are proud to know our daughter aided in the effort to free our land. We will bury her next to her brothers."

As her mother and father led the way, Hans, Hanta, Hazcra, Haisa, and Niltof carried the casket. The women softly sang a song which was usually sung when a Diwesh died in battle. Setting the casket down, each of the men took a turn digging the grave.

"Would you allow me to say a few words?" Hans asked before the casket was lowered into the grave.

"We would appreciate it," Dero assured him.

As everyone stood around the freshly dug grave, Hans thanked Nido for Arabella's bravery and unselfishness and entrusted her spirit into his care. Then the Diwesh lowered the casket into the grave, and each of them took a turn filling it in. When they were done, Ahe placed flowers upon the grave and the Diwesh silently returned to their sky sleds, leaving Reda and Dero to their grief.

* * *

They arrived in Berity the next day just in time to take part in the celebration. The official documents of government were signed, and everyone gathered together for feasting, music, and games. All the Diwesh joined in, and many of those who had taken part in the destruction of the Compounds took part in the telling and re-telling of the events of that night and the following days. The Diwesh were informed that the Runners had all left the country within two days after the Compounds had been destroyed. When evening came, there was a burning ceremony. All the Rasset mandated coverings were tossed on a bonfire and everyone cheered as they went up in flames.

The following morning the provisional new government, composed of the Council and six members of the Resistance, gathered to hear what had happened. When the Diwesh had finished relating all that had taken place Kye asked, "Why didn't you kill the Cibth and remove the danger of her ever again recruiting Olo and ruining lives?"

"First of all," Hans responded, "Diwesh do not kill prisoners. Those who are not killed in battle are not killed afterward. Secondly, should the Cibth escape the island, she will have a difficult time working her evil. The influence of a Cibth is largely due to their persuasiveness. Without a tongue, she will have a difficult time enlisting support for her schemes."

"What do you think will happen to the islands?" one of the Resistance leaders asked.

"Based on my calculations," Hazcra answered, "they will not come in contact with another land mass for at least a year and the islands Hepnet and the Cibth are on will take even longer. The probable route they will follow will take them to the Colder Regions where the Petick live—hardly easy victims for Cibth deceitfulness."

"Some would like you and your sons to stay and be a part of the new government," Yamam said, "including me."

"We are flattered, but must decline. This is the country of the Merene and those who rule should always be Merene. Niltof and Accebe will remain, as he is Merene and this is his homeland."

"If you will allow me to resume my position on the Council," Niltof said, "I would be honored to do so."

"As far as we are concerned," Dorla said, "you never ceased being on the Council."

"What of you and your family?" Yamam asked. "You are planning to stay with us, aren't you?"

"No, you do not need us any longer," Hans replied. "We will be leaving at sunrise."

"We will be indebted to you always," the members of the Resistance said in unison. "Know that you will be welcome here any time you should choose to return."

"Where are you going?" Vadi asked.

"Nido alone knows."

HELPFUL FACTS AND INFO

Merene—inhabitants of what became the Six Zones
    Vela—kept in Compounds to ensure treaty is kept
    Redere—Vela used to provide "special food" for Rasset
    Reth—Merene and others who are not Vela or Redere
    Resistance—made treaty with Rasset to avoid more destruction
    New Confederates—Merene freedom fighters

Rasset—average height, dark hair and eyes
    Leader
    Retona—heads of the Zones
    Dura—shaved heads—allowed to carry weapons

Runners—tall, with long legs. Used by Rasset to find escapees and troublemakers

Olo—pale eyes, square jaw, ears that protrude, head covered with fuzz.
    Afraid of dark
    Rahete and Reke
    Sasice and Kar
    Elacha and Sury

Diwesh
    Hans and Areboh
    Accebe and Niltof
    Hanta and Ahona
    Hazcra and Acir
    Ahe
    Haisa

Cibth—short with a pointed nose, large mouth, dark eyes, and ear lobes that hang down to their shoulders
    Raica

Petick—inhabitants of the Colder Regions

The Council—New Confederate ruling body
  Niltof
  Vadi
  Dorla
  Kye
  Yamam
  Neliv

The Demonstration—destroyed much land—a show of force to end any opposition
  Compound—where Vela are kept
  Underground—New Confederates headquarters
  Separation—division between Zones

Animals
  Neox—flying birds used for pulling sky sleds
  Scuzzets—brown and green fur, two inch teeth and sharp claws
  Sero—three-eyed horses used for heavy work
  Niso—raised for meat
  Bairan—small, swift horses only Rasset allowed to have

Plants
  Brallem bush—large, broad leaves collect enough water each day to keep a man alive
  Gusar trees—grow only in few locations along southern edge of mainland
  Curagena—needed to produce chooll
  Rohn bush—produces delicious berries, has thorns 1" or longer

Misc.
  Sky sleds—pulled by two Neox—used for transporting people
  Koieos—a sweet snack
  Chooll—made from sap of gusar trees mixed with grains from curagena
  Diwesh dagger—made of finest Diwesh steel